KT-434-150

ACC. No: 02879614

RANGELAND GUNS

Bradford Scott was a pseudonym for **Leslie Scott** who was born in Lewisburg, West Virginia. During the Great War, he joined the French Foreign Legion and spent four years in the trenches. In the 1920s he worked as a mining engineer and bridge builder in the western American states and in China before settling in New York. A bar-room discussion in 1934 with Leo Margulies, who was managing editor for Standard Magazines, prompted Scott to try writing fiction. He went on to create two of the most notable series characters in Western pulp magazines. In 1936, Standard Magazines launched, and in *Texas Rangers*, Scott under the house name of **Jackson Cole** created Jim Hatfield, Texas Ranger, a character whose popularity was so great with readers that this magazine featuring his adventures lasted until 1958. When others eventually began contributing Jim Hatfield stories, Scott created another Texas Ranger hero, Walt Slade, better known as *El Halcon*, the Hawk, whose exploits were regularly featured in *Thrilling Western*. In the 1950s Scott moved quickly into writing book-length adventures about both Jim Hatfield and Walt Slade in long series of original paperback Westerns. At the same time, however, Scott was also doing some of his best work in hardcover Westerns published by Arcadia House; thoughtful, well-constructed stories, with engaging characters and authentic settings and situations. Among the best of these, surely, are *Silver City* (1953), *Longhorn Empire* (1954), *The Trail Builders* (1956), and *Blood on the Rio Grande* (1959). In these hardcover Westerns, many of which have never been reprinted, Scott proved himself highly capable of writing traditional Western stories with characters who have sufficient depth to change in the course of the narrative and with a degree of authenticity and historical accuracy absent from many of his series stories.

RANGELAND GUNS

Bradford Scott

GUNSMOKE

This hardback edition 2011
by AudioGO Ltd
by arrangement with
Golden West Literary Agency

Copyright © 1989 by Leslie Scott.
Copyright © renewed 1988 by Lily Scott.
All rights reserved.

ISBN 978 1 445 85641 4

*This book is fiction. No resemblance is intended between any
character herein and any person, living or dead; any such
resemblance is purely coincidental.*

British Library Cataloguing in Publication Data available.

Printed and bound in Great Britain by
CPI Antony Rowe, Chippenham and Eastbourne

ONE

"THAT'LL BE FAR ENOUGH, STRANGER!"

Ranger Walt Slade, he whom the peons of the Rio Grande River villages named *El Halcon*, The Hawk, pulled Shadow, his tall black horse, to halt and regarded the lanky old farmer, a hint of amusement in his cold gray eyes.

The oldster held a rifle in his hands, held it at port, across his scrawny breast, and Slade's keen glance, which missed nothing, noted that the hammer was not at full cock.

"Oldtimer," he said in his deep, musical voice, "you'd be safer if you left that long-gun at home."

The old man stiffened. "Son," he replied grimly, "this rifle is loaded, and she means business."

"Just the same," Slade repeated, "you'd be safer if you didn't have it. I'll show you."

His slender, bronzed hands moved like the flicker of a hawk's wing, too swiftly for the eye to follow.

The farmer's jaw dropped, his eyes goggled, as he stared into the yawning muzzles, rock steady, of two long black guns that hadn't been there a split second before.

Slade flipped the big Colts. They turned a complete circle in the air, the plain black butts smacking against his palms, the muzzles rock steady as before. Then he holstered them with effortless ease and sat smiling at the old man, his even teeth flashing startlingly white in his bronzed face, his cold eyes suddenly sunny, the upward quirking of his rather wide mouth somewhat belying the hint of fierceness evinced in the prominent hawk nose and the long, powerful chin and jaw beneath.

The old man wet his suddenly dry lips with a nervous tongue, still staring unbelievingly at El Halcon; what had happened just couldn't happen!

5

"Son, I—I reckon you could have killed me, if you'd been of a mind to," he said a trifle dazedly.

"Yes," Slade nodded, "and the next man you try to stop might do just that. Folks in this section of Texas are practically born with guns in their hands and are inclined to take them seriously. Keep that in mind; and the next time you feel like talking turkey to someone, have your gun butt against your shoulder, and the hammer back. Even then you'd be taking a chance you shouldn't take unless absolutely necessary."

Abruptly the farmer saw the sunny eyes grow cold and narrow slightly. The music left the voice addressing him and was replaced by a steely note:

"Just what do you mean, anyhow, by stopping a peaceful stranger on an open trail the way you did?"

The old man hesitated. "We've been having a lot of trouble in this section of late, son," he said at last.

Ranger Walt Slade knew that without being told; it was the reason why he was in Vereda Valley not so far from the New Mexico line, but he only remarked casually,

"That so? How come?"

"It's mostly the Claxton fellers, but not them altogether," the farmer replied.

"The Claxtons?"

"Yes, they don't care over much for us farmers."

"Why not?"

The old man removed his battered hat and scratched his grizzled head.

"It's right smart of a story, I reckon," he replied. "You see, us farmers have been moving into this valley for the past year and better. Most of us came from Kentucky and Tennessee. We bought our land from the State, paid for it, got title. But Claxton and them other cattle raising fellers call us nesters and say we ain't got any right to be here. They say this valley has always been open range, as they call the land they use but ain't got title to, and that because it's always been open range it belongs to the cattlemen. The State said different when it sold us the land, but I reckon the cattlemen don't pay much attention to what folks over at the capital say. Anyhow, of late they've been raising heck and giving us a lot of trouble. They say we aim to take over the whole range country hereabouts, which just ain't so. Outside of this valley the land ain't over good for farming, though first rate for cattle raising."

Slade nodded. In his estimation, the old man was right on both scores.

"This valley never was used for cattle," the oldster went on. "It wasn't much good for anything but to grow weeds till us fellers brought water down from the hills and irrigated it. Now it grows first rate crops."

"And very likely would also grow good grass for cattle," Slade commented. "Did the trouble start right after you irrigated the land and made it productive?"

"No, not right away," the other said. "I reckon they didn't realize for a while how valuable the land had become once we got water onto it. At first they didn't seem to pay us no mind. Then all of a sudden they started saying that we aimed to take over the whole section and drive the cattle out. That just ain't the truth. We don't hanker for anything outside our valley; we've got all the land here we need. All we want is to be let alone and live our own lives in peace. But we can't make those fellers believe it. They've been accusing us of burning their hay stacks and stealing and poisoning their cattle."

The farmer paused to haul out an old black pipe and stuff it with tobacco. Slade took advantage of the opportunity to roll a cigarette with the slim fingers of his left hand.

"They been doing things to us, too, bad things," the oldster resumed. "Last week Jed Hargus was found dead in the bushes, shot between the eyes. The other fellers were stopped on the road and beat bad by ornery scuts with black rags tied over their faces. This road you're travelling runs straight through the valley and makes a short cut to the town down yonder—town named Vereda, same as the valley. Did you see where the road forked just before it entered the valley?" Slade nodded.

"The fork to the east heads for town, too, but it's considerable farther that way. We didn't object to the cattle

fellers using this road when things were peaceful. But of
late we've closed it and stop riders till we're sure they
don't mean any harm. That's why I stopped you just
now."

Slade nodded again, his eyes grave. He understood the
situation perfectly, had encountered its like before, and
knew that it was packed with dynamite. Here was the
making of a bloody range war such as Texas had known
all too often before. The eternal conflict between the
barons of the open range and the migrating tillers of the
soil who came to the West seeking homes and fresh
opportunity. But here appeared to be a new angle or
two that were puzzling. The cowmen, according to his
informant's story, had not tried to keep the farmers out
when they first appeared but had suddenly grown in-
imical to them after they improved the land by irrigation.
Which somehow to Slade's mind did not exactly make
sense and was opposed to rangeland thinking.

He glanced down the valley, which was long and com-
paratively narrow, walled in by bleak hills on either side.
Water or no water, it was not good cattle range. Would
be hard to work, and with plenty of good grazing land
to the north and east would hardly appear to offer tempta-
tion to the cowmen. Conversely, the land to the north
and east was not good farming land. Water was scarce,
and it was not amenable to irrigation, as was this low-
lying terrain between the flanking hills.

But he understood and appreciated the sentiment of
the ranchers. They feared the plow. Not one of them but
had known its devastating effect in other sections, where
cattle raising was concerned. The fenced farm was ana-
thema to them, a constant menace with its strands of
rusty barbed wire. Their fears, in this particular instance,
might be inconsistent and ungrounded, but it was a
genuine fear nevertheless.

Walt Slade, descended from ranching stock himself
and a product of the range, knew that emigration to the
West was not to be stopped. The farmers had been coming into Texas for years, now, and they would continue
to come; nothing could stop them. They were as tenacious

of purpose, as grimly fearless as the ranchers. Both breeds were in fact descended from common stock, both were imbued with the pioneering spirit, were accustomed to face difficulty and danger without flinching. It was flint on steel, and the sparks could well start a conflagration that would be devastating and hard indeed to stop. As a Texas Ranger it was his duty to smother the fire, if possible, before it really got going. For that purpose he was in Vereda Valley.

TWO

IN MOST CASES, SLADE KNEW, the enmity and the friction were utterly senseless. There was plenty of land for all, and usually the land which appealed to the farmers was not land best adapted for cattle raising, and vice versa. It looked like, on the surface at least, that this was the situation here. However, Slade held his judgment in abeyance until he could learn more of prevailing conditions.

"Our chief trouble," repeated the farmer, "is the Claxton fellers. Sid Claxton is the bellwether of the lot and he's mean as a barrel of snakes. He hates farmers, swears he's going to run the last one of us out of the section before he's finished with us. I'll say for him, though, he don't work under cover or wear a black cloth over his face."

The old man paused to relight his pipe. Slade smoked thoughtfully, his black brows drawing together in thought. He nodded to the other to proceed.

"The sheriff of the county don't help us much," the old man went on. "I'd say he sort of favors the cattlemen, which I reckon is natural, he being born and brought up in this country with them. We wrote a letter to Captain McNelty of the Rangers asking him to help us, but we ain't heard anything from him so far. Guess the Rangers are pretty busy, what with the trouble along the Border and all."

"I happen to know that Captain Jim never lets anybody down," Slade observed. "He will likely lend you a hand in a way you least expect."

"I hope so," said the farmer, "for things are kind of coming to a head and something real bad is likely to happen 'fore long. I hope not. All I hanker for is peace and a chance to farm."

His lined face suddenly looked very tired and old. He smiled up at the tall Ranger, a pathetic little smile with much of sadness in it.

"I worked hard down in Kentucky, but I couldn't get ahead," he continued. "The farm was plumb wore out and the payments on the mortgage came around mighty regular. My wife died down there—worked herself to death I reckon—and I sort of couldn't stand the place after that. So I sold out, managed to rake a few dollars together and came west along with the other fellers who hoped for something better, bringing my boy Nate with me. Lucky we did, too, as I'll tell you a little later, after I show you something. I figure you'd like Nate—he's almost as tall as you, but kind of gangling; didn't always eat over well when he was small, I'm afraid.

Slade's level eyes were all kindness. "I'm sure I'll like him," he said warmly. "Especially if he happens to be like what his dad appears to be."

The old man looked very pleased. "Tell you what, son," he said. "I got my horse tied over in the thicket. I'll get him and ride down the valley with you; that way you won't be stopped any more. We can stop off at my little house and have a bite to eat, and you can see Nate. Then you'll still have plenty of time to ride to town 'fore it gets dark, if that's where you're headed for. My name's Jethro Persinger."

"Be glad to," Slade said, introducing himself. He reached down and they gravely shook hands.

Persinger hooked his rifle over his arm, strode to a nearby thicket and in a moment reappeared riding a rawboned gray. Slade pinched out his cigarette butt, spoke to Shadow and together they headed down the narrow valley. They had covered less than a mile when Persinger jerked his thumb toward a gap in the cliffs to the left.

"That's where we get our water to irrigate with," he remarked. "There's a purty sizeable lake about four miles back in the hills; that gully leads right up to it, almost. Funny place; a big wall of rock holds the water in on this side. We looked it over while we were riding around hunting for a place to settle. My boy Nate figured out what to do," he added pridefully. "Nate had worked for some engineer fellers down in Tennessee who were building an irrigation dam and learned something about the business. He said we could cut right through the rock up near the top and still be a mite below the surface of the lake. We did it, and dug a channel down the gully to the valley. Doing that took about all our spare cash, but we got a good head of water, as you can see, and it ain't never failed us. The lake level remains just about the same the year round—fed by big springs that come up from down deep, I reckon."

Slade nodded his appreciation as he eyed the stream of clear water rushing down the gully in its stone lined channel. His interest in young Nate Persinger increased.

"A good piece of work," he commented. "Yes, very good. Your son has the makings of an engineer."

"He'd like to be one, but it takes money," replied Persinger. "Maybe some day, I hope."

"Strikes me as the sort who will make it some day," Slade said, and meant it. His gaze roved over the line of cliffs that marched solidly on either side of the valley, walling it in, with the hill crests looming above the beetling parapets of stone. Those on the east were perpendicular—a goat could not have climbed them; on the other hand, the western wall had a decided slant to it and was scored by rifts and washes.

The cliffs themselves were oddly striated, the great ribs of stone towering hundreds of feet into the air. Their predominant color was a pale gray, but there were bands and splotches of vivid green, chocolate brown and smoldering red.

Shortly before the death of his father, subsequent to financial reverses that entailed the loss of the elder Slade's ranch, Walt Slade had graduated from a famous college of engineering, planning to take a post graduate course to round out his education and better fit him for the profession he intended to make his life's work. That becoming impossible for the time being, he turned a receptive ear to Captain Jim McNelty, the Commander of the Border Battalion of the Texas Rangers, with whom he had worked some during summer vacations, when Captain Jim suggested that he come into the Rangers for a while and continue his studies in spare time. Long since he had acquired more from private study than he could have hoped for from the postgrad, but Ranger work had gotten a strong hold on him and he was loath to sever connections with the illustrious organization of law enforcement officers. Plenty of time to be an engineer; he'd stick with the Rangers for a while. Now he studied the frowning cliffs with a geologist's eye.

Feldspar, undoubtedly, both orthoclose and plagioclase, largely syenite, and they had undergone a great deal of weathering. Something about the unusual formation struck a responsive chord in his memory, just what he could not at the moment recall.

Soon after passing the aqueduct which brought the water from the hills they reached the cultivated lands. The crops were beautifully fresh and green in the morning sun. They were very good crops, Slade thought. Evidently the farmers had not overestimated the productiveness of the land once it was enriched with ample water.

They passed men working the fields or standing in the doorways of the little farmhouses. All had a cordial nod and greeting for old Jethro Persinger; but they were silent as they gazed at his companion whose garb and riding gear obviously proclaimed him a cowboy.

Persinger's house was far down the valley. Young Nate turned out to be a larger edition of his father. He had a shy smile and a quiet, reserved manner that appealed to Slade. Also, he quickly proved his ability to rustle a prime helpin' of chuck on short notice. They lingered over the meal and the sun was slanting down the western sky when Slade rode away, headed for Vereda, the cattle town just south of the valley mouth. He wondered whimsically what would be his reception there.

Due to his habit of working undercover whenever possible and often not revealing his Ranger connections, Walt Slade had built up a peculiar dual reputation. Those who knew the truth were wont to declare that he was the ablest as well as the most fearless of the Rangers. Others who knew only his exploits, including some puzzled sheriffs and marshals, insisted, often profanely, that he was just a blasted outlaw too smart to get caught. Slade did nothing to discourage this erroneous viewpoint, although he well knew that it laid him open to grave personal danger. On the other hand it opened up avenues of information that would have been closed to a known peace officer. So as El Halcon he went his carefree way, satisfied with the present and giving scant thought to the future.

The lovely blue dusk was softing down from the hills when Slade reached Vereda. The eastern crags were bathed in a soft glow and the rugged battlements to the west were ringed about with saffron flame. Windows had changed from darkly staring eyes to squares and rectangles of ruddy gold. Atop poles, lanterns that served as street lights began to wink as an old Mexican with a ladder touched flame to the wicks. The board sidewalk of the main street resounded to the clump of boots that provided a solid undertone to the whirl and patter of words, the bawling of song and the whine of fiddles that drifted over the swinging doors of saloon and dance hall and gambling emporium.

Slade saw many cowhands in careless but efficient range attire much like his own—Levis, the bibless overalls the cowboy favored, soft shirts, vivid handkerchiefs looped about sinewy throats, battered, broad-brimmed "J.B.'s", half-boots, high of heel, of softly tanned leather, and the ubiquitous cartridge belt and Colt or Smith & Wesson Forty-five.

There was a considerable sprinkling of Mexicans, some in tattered overalls, bare of foot, their unkempt hair topped by enormous sombreros incrusted with silver.

Others were darkly picturesque in short jackets, and tight pantaloons of black velvet likewise adorned with silver conchas.

Riders clicked along, their horses' irons kicking up puffs of dust. There was a smell of sweat, horseflesh, of the singed hair of cattle. To the south, curving around the town, gleamed the twin steel ribbons of a railroad. Even as Slade rode into town a train roared westward without pausing, leaving behind it a swirl of smoke and the pungent tang of hot oil, sulphur and creosote. Following the line of the railroad with his eyes, Slade noted extensive loading pens and a number of sidings. The town evidently rated importance as a cattle shipping point.

"And she's got the looks and sound of a hell raiser," Slade remarked to Shadow as he pulled up in front of a livery stable marked by a swinging sign. Shadow snorted cheerful agreement and looked expectant as his rider leaned over and banged on the door.

"Sure I can put him up," said the crusty old stable keeper who answered the knock. "Where can you get a room and a surroundin'? The Diamond Flush saloon right around the corner puts out good chuck and the drinks and the gals are average. They got rooms on the second floor to rent out. I sleep there. Clean, and no bugs. Just tell the barkeep you want one and he'll sign you up. Nope, you don't have to pay me in advance; a jigger who rides a horse like that one and is friends with him don't need no more rec'mendation to me. Horse will be here when you want him—I got a Sharpe's buffalo gun that says so. Easy, boy, don't lay your ears back at me; I'm your amigo!" This last to Shadow, who glanced questioningly at Slade and then thrust his velvety muzzle into the gnarled old hand and blew softly.

"Reckon you two just have to look at each other to know what's what," chuckled the keeper as he heaped a feedbox with oats. "There's a trough of nice cold water in the back if you'd care for a sluice to pry the dust off. Soap and towel handy. My name's Hastings, Bert Hastings. Tell 'em at the saloon that I sent you."

Slade thanked the hospitable keeper, greatly enjoyed the

sluice in the icy water and after combing his thick black hair, set out for the Diamond Flush. He left his rig behind, taking with him only one saddle pouch which contained some necessaries.

He had the luck to catch a drink juggler at the end of the bar and to him broached the business of a room, mentioning Bert Hasting's name.

"Sure you can have one," replied the barkeep. "Miguel," he called to an old Mexican swamper who was pottering about with a mop and a broom, "Miguel, show this gent to—let's see—Number Five; you have the keys."

The swamper straightened up, his eyes widened and he bowed his head reverently.

"Come, Capitan," he said, employing the Mexican title of respect. He led the way up an outside stair and to a room a few doors down a hall from the stairhead. Opening the door, he passed Slade the key.

"There will be warm water for washing and shaving in the morning," he said.

Slade offered him a peso, but the old fellow shook his head smilingly.

"I could not allow money to come between me and El Halcon, the friend of the lowly," he said softly.

"Thank you," Slade said. Spotted already! Well, it might be for the best. He placed the saddle pouch under the bed in the comfortable looking room and returned to the saloon in quest of a drink and a bite to eat.

The Diamond Flush was a big place and typically cow country. There was a long bar, tables for diners, a lunch counter for folks who wanted their chuck in a hurry, a faro bank, two roulette wheels, a number of poker tables, all doing business, a rather large dance floor and an orchestra. Recalling Bert Hastings' remark, Slade decided the girls on the floor were a bit better than average. As to the drinks, his judgment must be held in abeyance until he tasted one.

The long bar was crowded, but Slade observed an open space next to a bad tempered looking individual with graying hair and almost as tall as himself and even broader. He edged his way toward the opening, slipped on a wet

cigar butt and lunged against the big man just as he was
raising a drink to his lips.

There was a click of glass striking hard against teeth, a
splatter of spilled whiskey and a roaring curse. The big
man whirled like a cat, seized Slade in a grip that numbed
his arms and hurled him violently back. As Slade reeled,
the other, his blocky face contorted with passion, flipped
a gun from its holster with effortless ease.

THREE

CAUGHT OFF BALANCE AND UNPREPARED as he
was, Slade's guns were out first, yawning hungrily at the
other. But before either could make a further move, a man
was between them, a tall, shapely man with a handsome,
hard-lined face. His hand slammed the burly oldster's gun
down till the muzzle pointed to the floor. "Pen those hog-
legs and look behind you!" he snapped over his shoulder
at Slade.

From the corner of his eyes, El Halcon had already seen
the four bartenders coming up with sawed-off shotguns
in their hands. He sheathed his Colts and stood waiting.
The man between spoke to his opponent, his voice quiet,
modulated but menacingly forceful.

"Sid Claxton, what the devil's the matter with you?" he
said. "Do you always have to go off half-cocked like a
trigger-happy fool? This young fellow didn't aim to jostle
your elbow. It was an accident, as you would have realized
if you'd use your head for something other than to hold
up your hat."

"Reckon you're right, Webb," Claxton conceded surlily,
"but if you'd had your front teeth half knocked out and
your eyes burning from that rattler juice you sell for
whiskey, maybe you wouldn't have took it cool and easy.
And I didn't aim to shoot him; I just wanted to get the
drop on him before he shot me. The way those guns of
his are slung means business."

"A lot of good it would have done you," snapped Webb. "He'd have killed you about three times before you could pull trigger. Sometimes I think you haven't the brains of a sheepherder."

Claxton opened his lips to voice an angry reply, but at that moment about a hundred-and-ten pounds of wildcat landed on him. A wildcat in the very shapely shape of a girl with flaming red hair, a red mouth and very big and very blue eyes.

"So you're at it again!" she cried. "Can't I leave you alone for an hour without you getting into trouble!"

She seized him by one big ear and gave his head a vigorous shake.

"Stop it!" he bawled. "That hurts!"

"It'll hurt more if you don't learn to behave yourself," she assured him, giving him another shake that brought a bellow of pain.

Snickers ran over the room. Slade leaned against the bar and laughed till the tears hopped down his bronzed cheeks. The girl whirled on him.

"What do you see that's so funny?" she demanded. "Can't I—" Her voice trailed off.

Slade said nothing, only smiled down at her from his great height. The big eyes widened. A wave of color mantled her cheeks and the white forehead beneath the rebellious curly red hair. She turned back to Sid Claxton, whose ear she still held.

"You're going home," she said.

"All right! all right!" he agreed sheepishly, "only please let go my ear; it's getting sore." He looked over her head, met Slade's dancing eyes and grinned, a grin that abruptly caused his bad tempered old face to greatly resemble the girl's and greatly change its expression.

"Sorry I laid my paws on you," he said, "and listen, son, don't ever get married. See what comes of it?"

"I'd say what evidently came of yours would be an inducement to any man to get married in a hurry," Slade replied smilingly.

"Everyone to their taste, as the old lady said when she kissed the cow," returned Claxton. "Hope to see you again, son, and then we'll have a drink together with no wimmen around to bother us. All right, Verna, I'm coming." He gently disengaged her slim fingers from his ear and tucked her arm through his.

At the swinging doors, Verna Claxton glanced over her shoulder and smiled, her even little teeth flashing white against the scarlet of her lips. Slade waved with his hand and turned to face Webb, who was regarding him with a peculiar expression in his dark eyes.

"The only person in the world who can handle him when he's got his mad up," he remarked, jerking his thumb toward the door. "She can wrap him around her finger any time."

"A rancher?" Slade asked casually.

"Yes," nodded Webb. "He owns the Cross C, the biggest and best spread in the section. He sort of runs the section and has for a good many years. Well, have one on the house," he added, motioning to a bartender. "Be seeing you." With a nod he departed to attend to his many duties.

The bartender who poured Slade's drink was a bustling individual with a ferocious scowl.

"Good thing you did what the boss told you to," he rumbled. "I had my scattergun lined on you. In another second I'd have—"

"Died," Slade finished for him.

The barkeep looked startled, started to answer; but apparently something in the steady eyes boring into his changed his mind. He turned away with a mumble. Slade sipped his drink and absently studied the room in the back bar mirror, for his thoughts were elsewhere.

So that was Sid Claxton, the leader of the ranchers in their row with the farmers, according to Jethro Persinger. A salty customer, all right. Slade was familiar with the type, a successful baron of the open range, arrogant, intolerant, self-sufficient, but he looked honest. Although his notions of honesty might be peculiar and founded largely on his own personal opinions and prejudices.

The swinging doors flung open, and the man who occupied his thoughts reappeared, still holding his daughter's arm; he strode straight to where Slade stood.

"There ain't no figuring women," he said resignedly. "Now she's decided she wants something to eat before heading for home, and that I should have that drink with you to show there's no hard feelings."

"Fine!" Slade applauded, smiling at the little redhead, who smiled back with a flash of her big eyes; he beckoned a bartender.

"I'm going to sit at that vacant table over by the window," Miss Verna announced. "You two can join me after you finish your drink. Don't be too long; I'm starved."

"Me, too," said Claxton. "How about you, son?"

"I was just thinking of having a bite," Slade admitted.

They downed their drink, clicking glasses, and joined Verna at the table. All three were hungry and they had an enjoyable dinner.

"Blaine Webb sure knows how to put on a good surroundin'," Claxton said as with a sigh of contentment he pushed back his empty plate. "Because of it he does a big daytime business, which is sort of unusual for these rumholes. A smart man, Webb, and he keeps order, as you may have noticed a while back."

"Decidedly so," Slade agreed with a smile.

At that moment Webb himself came over and occupied a vacant chair.

"One on the house to top off with," he said. "You'll have wine, Verna?"

"A small glass," the girl replied. "That's my limit, one glass of wine after dinner."

"Your complexion attests to that," Slade observed.

She colored prettily and flashed him a glance from her blue eyes.

"Thank you," she said demurely. "Do you know, sir, that you as yet haven't told us your name?"

Slade laughingly supplied it. "Plumb slipped me," he said. "Your Dad took to calling me son, and it seemed sort of natural for him to do so."

"Oh, I could be your dad, all right," Claxton said. "I'm past fifty. Verna's just turned twenty-one."

"Dad, a lady's age is supposed to be a secret," his daughter chided.

"Never could see no sense to it," Claxton replied cheerfully. "There ain't no setting back the clock."

"Nor to try to make the hands stand still," Slade observed. "Even though you destroy the wheels, the hands keep moving. Folks try it now and then, but it won't work."

Old Sid looked puzzled, but Blaine Webb nodded his understanding.

"Emphatically so, Mr. Slade," he said. "That's what I tell some folks every now and then; they'd do better to listen. By the way, Sid, what got you so on the prod tonight? When you came in you looked riled as a centipede with chilblains."

"Reckon you'd have been riled, too, if you'd just seen what I saw this afternoon," growled Claxton. "Nigh onto a dozen prime beef steers stiff and swelled up alongside a poisoned waterhole. Blast those nesters, anyhow! I'll run the last one of those hellions out of this section 'fore I'm finished. See if I don't!"

"How can you be so sure the nesters did it?" Webb objected.

"Who else, I'd like to know?" Claxton countered belligerently. Webb shrugged his broad shoulders.

"There are people who wouldn't be averse to doing you a bad turn, and you know it," he replied. "You have a genius for getting folks on the prod against you. And as for running out the farmers, there you are trying to stop the hands of the clock. Try it and you may very likely bite off more than you can comfortably chew. They're not the sort you can push around with impunity; they're salty. For your own safety, it would be better to steer clear of them."

Claxton flushed darkly and his eyes sparkled with anger. "Meaning to suggest I'm scared of the hellions?" he demanded.

Webb shrugged again. "I'm saying what I have for your own good and safety, that's all," he answered.

"I ain't ever seen the man I was scared of, and I sure ain't going to start with nesters," old Sid growled. "So—"

"I think," Verna interrupted, "that this discussion has

continued long enough for the time being. Suppose we change the subject. Mr. Slade, do you dance?"

"I can manage to fall over my own feet when nobody else's are in the way," Slade replied.

"All right, let's see how gracefully you can fall over them," she said. "Blaine, will you please ask the orchestra leader to play a waltz the next number?"

"Be glad to," Webb answered, rising to his feet and crossing the room with his swinging, assured stride.

"I hope you won't think me forward, but I wanted to get them separated," the girl said in low tones as they walked to the floor and waited for the number to end. "Whenever they get together they start discussing the trouble with the farmers. Dad immediately gets angry, especially when Blaine reminds him of the danger he'll incur from trouble with the farmers. Blaine may be right. Those men strike me as not the kind one can affront with impunity. Besides, I don't like the whole affair. They are human like the rest of us and have a right to live. I hope you agree with me."

"I do, definitely," Slade assured her, adding, "And perhaps your father will also end up feeling that way."

"I hope so," she replied. "Yes, I hope so. Here's our number!"

At the table, old Sid lit his pipe and settled back comfortably in his chair to watch the dancing.

"That young feller is in for a surprise," he chuckled aloud. "My little gal's the best dancer in this end of Texas."

FOUR

However, it was Sid Claxton himself who got the surprise, so much so that a moment later found him sitting bolt upright in his chair, staring.

For in the tall Ranger, Miss Verna had found a partner fitted to her undoubted gift for dancing. Gradually the other couples edged away from them, until they had

practically the whole floor for their performance, and when
the number ended there was a general shout of applause
and a clapping of hands, stomping of feet and hammering
with glasses on the bar.

"You're wonderful!" Verna exclaimed breathlessly. "I
never met anyone like you."

"I fear, then, you haven't met many," Slade smiled.

"Oh, no? Well, I have, and I stand by what I said.
You're a wonderful dancer. Hello, Estaban, what do you
want?" This to the orchestra leader, who was beside them,
bowing and smiling and holding out a guitar.

"I want that *El Capitan* shall sing for us," Estaban replied in his precise English. "For, *Senorita*, he sings as he
dances, most wonderful."

"Please do, Mr. Slade," Verna begged. "If Estaban says
you can, you can."

"Under one condition, that you stop Mistering me,"
Slade agreed. "It grows monotonous, and I think you
caught my first name."

"All right—Walt," she replied, blushing a little. "And
I think you heard Dad call my name, did you not?"

"Guess I did—Verna," Slade answered. "Okay, here
goes."

He accepted the guitar and ran his fingers over the strings
with crisp power. Glancing about he noted that cowhands
were in the majority, so he stepped to the edge of the plat-
form, threw back his black head and sang them a rollicking
old ballad of the range——

> "I'm headin' for a rangeland
>   Where there ain't no corral bars;
>   Down the Milky Way I'm ridin'
>   Through the sunset, herdin' stars,
>   Where the Little Bear's a-sleepin'
>   While his Big Bear mammy sings,
>   As I amble past 'em, forkin'
>   A pinto hoss with wings!

There's young Mercury sparkin' Venus
While ol' red-eyed Mars, her pap,
With a plumb skinful of moonshine,
Is a-takin' him a nap.
And the Dog Star comes a-waggin',
A-follered by his Pup,
As a maverickin' comet
Tries to dodge the Last Round-up!"

The music ended with a crash of chords and Slade stood smiling as an even greater roar of applause shook the rafter, and shouts were heard of "Give us another, feller, give us another!"

Slade glanced down at the small girl who was regarding him wide-eyed, turned to the expectant gathering and sang a hauntingly beautiful, tremulously sad love song of Old Spain.

And as the great golden bass-baritone pealed and thundered through the room, there was a hush as before a shrine, and more than one hardened oldtimer brushed a horny hand across his eyes. Perhaps cigarette smoke had gotten into them! While the dance floor girls let the tears fall unashamed.

In a last exquisite breath of melody the music died—

"And there beyond the sunset
I'll be waiting, dear, for you!"

And the silence that followed was a tribute to the tall singer of dreams greater than the loudest applause.

Slade handed the guitar to its owner, who bowed low, and, Verna clinging to his arm, walked back to where old Sid waited, his eyes suspiciously bright.

"Son," the rancher asked heavily, "did you say you're a cowhand?"

"When I'm working at it," Slade smiled. Claxton shook his head.

"I don't see why," he said. "I don't see why! But if you are and looking for a place to coil your twine, there's one waiting for you over to my Cross C spread. And," he added with a grin, "I'll be willing to pay you a mite better'n regulation wages if you'll promise to sing for me now and then."

"Thank you, sir," Slade replied. "I'm likely to take you up on it, a little later."

"Please, do," Verna urged.

Old Sid glanced at the clock over the bar. "Reckon it's time to hit the hay," he remarked. "Too late to ride back to the spread tonight, so we'll amble over to the Cowman's Hotel and sign up for a couple of rooms. I usually pound my ear upstairs over the saloon when I stay in, but it's hardly a place for a gal, what with the racket down here and all. Walk to the hotel with us, son?"

"Be glad to," Slade answered. They left the saloon together, curious eyes following their progress, among them Blaine Webb's whose brows drew together as if in thought, once again the peculiar expression shadowing his ruggedly handsome face as he observed Verna snuggling close to Slade, one slender hand on his arm possessively.

"That was just about the finest looking couple I ever saw on a dance floor," an oldtimer standing nearby remarked to Webb. "I got a notion," he added with a chuckle, "that Claxton's little gal is sorta going for that young feller. Can't blame her, though, if she does. He's sure nice looking and a feller who can dance and sing like that just sorta makes a gal roll her eyes."

"But she could be making a serious mistake," Webb replied. "She doesn't know anything about him, where he came from, what he is."

"Looks okay to me," the other stated emphatically.

"Yes, but looks can sometimes be deceptive," Webb said. "Excuse me, I want to have a word with Estaban." He crossed the room and engaged the orchestra leader in conversation, and as Estaban spoke, the furrow between Blaine Webb's eyes deepened and took on what might have been interpreted as a worried look.

The walk to the Cowman's Hotel was short, but Slade found it enjoyable.

"Son, I hope you'll ride out to see us soon," old Sid said as they paused in the office. "You can't miss my casa. Just take the northeast trail out of town and follow it for about eight miles. My house is the second one you come to, the big one in a grove. The first you pass is Blaine Webb's Diamond W. It's smaller than mine and set back farther from the trail."

"Webb is a rancher as well as a saloonkeeper?" Slade remarked.

"That's right. Him and his partner, Rex Masters, bought it from old Tom Haggerty about a year back. Tom was getting sort of old and his daughter over in east Texas wanted him to come and live with her. It ain't a big holding, but it's a good one and convenient to town. Masters does most of the work of running it. He's in the Diamond Flush some in the daytime. Nice feller, gets along well with everybody. One of those real soft-spoke gents who's always smiling. Webb's smart, all right, but I've a notion Masters is even smarter. Blaine listens to what he has to say. Well, I crave a mite of shuteye. Wait a minute."

He lumbered to the desk and wrote in the register. "Your room is Number Nine, chick," he said to Verna. "I got Number Twelve, down the hall. Good night, son, we'll be riding early in the morning. Don't forget, we'll be expecting you." With a wave of his hand, he stamped up the stairs.

"Really, I'm not at all sleepy," Verna said. "How'd you like to take a little walk? It's a beautiful night."

"I'd like nothing better, unless—it would be to stop somewhere for a while," Slade replied.

She glanced up at him, her eyes dancing. "You're precipitate," she said, with a little musical trill of laughter. "But the way I've been forcing myself on you all evening, I guess I have no right to complain, and—I have no intention of doing so. How's that?"

Slade chuckled. "I know just how a jigger with a busted flush feels when his bluff is called by four aces," he replied. They laughed together and walked out arm-in-arm.

It was a beautiful night and they strolled slowly along the main street, to the south, in silence for a while.

"Walt," she suddenly said, "I don't think I ever knew my father to take to anyone on short notice as he has to you. Usually he is chary of intercourse with strangers—

perhaps suspicious would be the better word—and about all they can get out of him is a grunt. With you he at once began to talk freely. He felt very bad over losing his temper with you at the bar. I knew it, and knew he was anxious to make amends, although he didn't say so. That's one of the reasons why I insisted that he go back and have a drink with you."

"What was the other reason?" Slade asked.

"Well," she replied frankly, "I was curious about you. I might as well admit it. And a woman with unsatisfied curiosity is not a happy woman."

"And is it satisfied now?" he asked, his voice grave but his eyes alight with laughter.

"Not at all," she admitted. "I still can't figure you, as Dad would express it. Although you evasively conceded to him that you are a cowhand, I know very well that you are not, although doubtless you've worked on spreads. Chambermaiding cows is not your vocation, of that I am positive. Just what you are I don't know, but I'll find out. A woman always has ways of finding out things, if she really wants to."

"Under certain circumstances," he smilingly conceded.

The very big and very blue eyes rose slowly to meet his, and their expression was inscrutable. And Walt Slade found it more than a little disquieting.

"I'll—find—out," she said softly, her hand tightening on his arm.

"What you learn may not please you," he retorted.

"Perhaps not," she conceded. "For often a woman learns things about a man that may not altogether please her, his lack of interest in herself, for instance."

"I don't think you need bother on that score, where any man is concerned," he replied with conviction.

"Then why worry at all?" she laughed. "At least, where you are concerned, nothing I may learn, or hear, will perturb me."

"There you may be making a serious mistake," he returned gravely.

"No!"

"Why so positive?"

"A woman's intuition, perhaps, but there is one thing I fear I may learn," she added, her voice a trifle wistful.

"What?"

"Remember the last lines in your song? I do fear that I may learn that you are a man who's always riding toward the sunset."

"Aren't we all?"

"Yes, metaphorically speaking, but not always imbued with an intense desire to see what is there, or what's over the next hilltop."

Slade hardly knew how to answer that one; there was too much truth in it, where his own case was concerned.

They had passed beyond the outskirts of the town and paused on the bank of a small star-dimpled stream.

"It didn't used to be here," the girl said, gesturing to the hurrying water.

"The overflow from the farmers' irrigation project?"

"That's right."

"Must be to the advantage of the spreads to the north, quite a volume of water there," Slade commented.

"Yes, it is," she replied. "It runs across Blaine Webb's holding and across ours. But Dad is afraid of it. He says the farmers can poison it."

"Ridiculous!" the Ranger scoffed. "Running water purifies itself within a few miles. If all the arsenic in Texas were dumped into it up in the valley it would still be drinkable here."

"I know," she said, "but I can't convince Dad. He says somebody told him it could be done."

"Do you happen to know who that somebody is?" Slade asked with interest.

She shook her head, her glowing hair catching glints from the starlight. "He didn't mention the name, just said it was somebody smart who'd know what he was talking about."

"Yes, quite likely somebody very smart," Slade agreed dryly. She glanced at him inquiringly, but he did not elaborate on his remark.

"It's nice here, after the noise and smoke, don't you think?" she said.

"Yes," he replied, "very nice. Would you like to stay for a while?"

"I would," she said as she raised her face. Her eyes were softly slumbrous, her lips sweet.

Quite some time later they walked slowly back to the hotel, and the hand on his arm was even more possessive than before.

FIVE

SLADE WENT TO BED in his room over the Diamond Flush in a fairly complacent frame of mind. Things were working out better than he had hoped. He had gotten in touch with a representative of the farmers who appeared to be reliable and had gotten their side of the story from him. In addition, he had contacted the leader of the ranchers in quite a satisfactory manner and with pleasing results. To say nothing of also having met and become decidedly friendly with Sid Claxton's very charming daughter. All in all, he figured he'd gotten off to a good start. Suppressing the trouble building up in the section might not be too difficult after all.

After a good night's rest, he arose around mid morning. A knock on the door caused him to open it. There was old Miguel, the swamper, with a large container of hot water.

"I have been listening, and when I heard you move I fetched the water for washing and shaving," the old fellow explained.

"That's mighty nice of you, Miguel," Slade replied.

"It is a great honor to serve El Halcon," Miguel said with a smile and a bob of his gray head as he turned and pattered down the stairs.

Finding himself decidedly hungry, Slade descended to the Diamond Flush in quest of some breakfast. Blaine Webb was not in evidence, but another man of authority was, a slender, elegant man of somewhat above middle height who seemed to move on springs, so graceful and assured was his walk. He had finely formed features, dark hair inclined to curl, and very clear eyes of very pale blue. He nodded to Slade in a friendly manner and a little later approached his table.

"Mr. Slade, is it not?" he asked in a pleasantly modulated voice. "I am Rex Masters, half owner of this place. I was told about you this morning by my old amigo Sid Claxton. It would appear that you and Mr. Claxton became quite friendly after a—slight disagreement."

"Yes, we got along all right, thanks largely to the timely intervention of your partner, Mr. Webb," Slade replied.

"A fine man, Mr. Claxton," Masters said. "Sort of apt to paw sand sometimes, but honest as they come, and I think he has a kind heart under a bristly exterior."

"Wouldn't be surprised if you're right," Slade conceded. "Gets ringey in a hurry but cools down quickly."

"Especially if he's shown he is in the wrong," Masters nodded. "Hope you'll see fit to stay with us for a while, Mr. Slade." With a smile and a nod he walked back to the bar. And watching the set of his head and shoulders and his assured manner, Slade thought that "Masters" was not a misnomer, nor even "Rex", for that matter. Without a doubt, Blaine Webb's partner was something of a personality.

After finishing his breakfast and a leisurely cigarette, Slade strolled out onto the main street. He had not walked to the first corner when he saw two gangling figures headed toward him. With a smile, he recognized old Jethro Persinger and his son Nate.

The farmers greeted El Halcon with warmth. "Was figuring to ride up through the hills to where the water comes down from the lake," Jethro announced. "We have to pack a load of supplies to the shack up there where the boys stand guard over the flume, for if the cattle fellers took a notion to cut it they would cause us a world of trouble and considerable expense. So we can't afford to take chances. How'd you like to come along and keep us company, son? Sort of interesting place up there—never saw anything just exactly like it."

"I'll be glad to," Slade accepted the invitation. "I'll get my horse."

They rounded the corner together, and from the door of the Diamond Flush, Rex Masters followed them with his pale eyes, and looked very thoughtful.

Half an hour later, Slade and the Persingers rode out of town headed due north. A lead mule packed the needed supplies. A few miles to the north, the trail turned and climbed into the hills, a narrow track that while undoubtedly very old, showed few signs of recent usage.

"The town takes its name from this trace," remarked Jethro. "They tell me Vereda is Mexican talk for trail. That's all the Mexicans ever called this trace, I've heard. Just called it The Trail and let it go at that. A feller said outlaws and cattle stealers used it a lot in the old days. Wouldn't be surprised if they use it some yet. The cattle-men to the north say they've been losing cattle of late. Of course they blame us farmers, but who ever heard of a farmer stealing cattle. Wouldn't know how to handle 'em, what to do with 'em or where to take 'em. About all us fellers know about cattle is from handling a few milk cows and a bull now and then. I wouldn't want to try to do anything with one of those rambunctious longhorns. This trace bends through the hills and across to New Mexico, I've heard. Never followed it that far."

Slade nodded. He suspected that the old trail did afford a quick route to the wilder New Mexico hills, where there was always a ready market for widelooped cows.

The trail bored on through the hills, twisting and turn-ing, dipping into ravines, skirting the edge of dizzy cliffs, furtive, snake-like, seeming to avoid the full light of day whenever possible, always seeking the shadow. Gaunt shoulders of naked stone edged close to it, and tangled thickets which would have afforded concealment for a hundred riders. The boulders that studded its surface were scarred and blackened, as if from the slash of whizzing lead and the slow drip of drying blood.

"Another couple of miles and she slides over to the edge of the cliffs to follow 'em north and you can see down into the valley," said Jethro after they had proceeded for perhaps half a score of miles along the lonely track.

Soon afterward the trail curved sharply to the west, the angle slowly widening. A heavier bristle of growth appeared, doubtless fringing the lip of the wall which hemmed the valley in on the east, the cliffs of which he had noted in the course of his ride to Vereda were unbroken and perpendicular.

Suddenly Slade tensed in an attitude of listening. From somewhere ahead, faint with distance, like the crackle of burning sticks under a pot, came a stutter of gun fire.

"Somebody shooting," muttered Jethro. "That's funny. Listen to it keep up!"

Slade's hand tightened on the bridle. He spoke a quiet word to Shadow and the tall horse lengthened his stride. The Persingers urged their mounts to greater effort and the trio rode swiftly toward the loudening reports.

Abruptly the trail veered more sharply to the west; they brushed through a straggle of thicket and the valley floor lay before them, far below. Slade's hand tightened on the bridle again and Shadow halted so quickly that the Persingers' mounts jostled against him as they hauled back on the reins. Old Jethro uttered a sharp exclamation.

Grim tragedy was in the making down there on the valley floor. In the middle of a meadow a man lay sprawled on his face, his limbs outflung, his body limp and distorted. Partly concealed in the grass lay other men from whom came spurts of bluish smoke. The crack of their guns drifted thinly to the cliff tops. And from ahead, beyond the tangle of growth through which the trail ran, came other reports, louder reports, evenly spaced, as if riflemen were taking slow and deliberate aim.

"The skunks are holed up on the cliff tops ambushing the boys!" exclaimed old Jethro. He urged his horse ahead, but Slade seized the bit strap in an iron grip and jerked the snorting animal to a halt.

"Hold it!" he snapped. "Do you want to ride into a drygulching? Back! and around through the chaparral. Steady now, we've got to get behind them. If they sight us first we'll have about as much chance as a rabbit in a hound dog's mouth."

Muttering and mumbling, Jethro obeyed. His silent son said nothing, and fingered the lock of his rifle.

Leading the way for a hundred yards or so back along the trail, Slade turned Shadow's head to the tangle of mesquite and other thorny growth. It was hard going through the chaparral and the Persingers' horses snorted their anger and disgust. Their riders maintained a grim silence despite the raking of thorns and twigs. Shadow, worming his way through narrow holes, was voiceless as his master.

Soon the crackle of shots atop the cliff was directly opposite. Slade pulled up, listened a moment and gestured for silence.

"Leave the horses here," he directed in a whisper, swinging to the ground. "We'll have to cover the rest of the distance on foot; they'd hear the horses coming through the brush and be set for us. Quiet, now, don't break any rotten branches or kick stones, and hope the cayuses will keep quiet; I wish Nate were riding a gelding instead of a mare. Female horses are uncertain. Come along, if we have luck we should catch them settin'."

Silently they glided through the brush, drawing nearer and nearer the sound. A final fringe of growth and they reached a little clearing which flanked the cliff. Directly ahead, perhaps twenty paces distant, crouched five men, well hidden from the farmers below by a swell of stone which formed the cliff lip; they were sighting and firing into the valley.

Slade drew his guns, motioned to his companions to wait; he was a law officer and must give the hellions a chance to surrender. Stepping into the clearing, he opened his lips to speak. And at that instant Nate Persinger's mare neighed shrilly.

The drygulchers whirled at the sound, flinging their rifles to the front; the clearing rocked to a bellow of gunfire.

Slade felt lead fan his face. A slug streaked a line of red along the angle of his jaw, sending him reeling for an instant with the shock. Another plucked at his sleeve like an urgent hand. Through the rattling crash of his own guns he could hear the banging of his companions' rifles.

Three men went down at that first thundering volley. The remaining two fought back viciously like cornered rats; and like cornered rats they died, under a hail of lead.

Slade strode across the clearing, the Persingers at his heels, rifles cocked and ready for action. However, their precaution was needless. Four of the drygulchers were dead, the fifth still alive but going fast. Slade knelt beside the dying man; glazing, hatefilled eyes glared into his; curses bubbled through the blood froth on the sagging lips. The drygulcher's chest arched mightily as he fought frantically for air; he expelled his breath in a whistling gasp and went limp. A hard man to the last.

"Well, none of them will tell us anything," Slade remarked. "At least of their own accord," he added as he proceeded to systematically examine the bodies.

Three of the drygulchers were hard-case individuals in well worn range clothes. The other two also boasted cowhand garb, but the clothes were new and showed little sign of use. He turned out the pockets of all five and discovered nothing of significance save a rather large sum of money which he passed to Jethro Persinger, saying,

"I guess the dead man down below left dependents who will need it more than the country treasury, where it'll go if we turn it in." He proceeded to give the dead men's hands a careful once-over.

"Come here, both of you," he said. "Take a look at the hands of this pair in new clothes. Look close, especially at the fingertips, and tell me what you see."

"Why," said old Jethro, "they look sorta pink and thin-skinned."

"I know what it is!" young Nate exclaimed triumphantly. "I've heard tell of it. The fingertips were rubbed with sandpaper to make 'em sensitive, so that a feller can feel markings on cards when he's dealing."

"Good eyes," Slade said. "Yes, you hit it square on the nailhead. These two hellions were gamblers, not cowhands as they posed to be in case somebody got a look at them.

The other three were cowhands, once upon a time, but not recently. Look close again and you can see the scars left by rope and branding iron quite a while back. Remember what you've seen, but don't talk about it. Understand?"

"Guess we do, and we'll keep our traps shut," said Jethro. "Don't know why you ask it, but we'll do as you say." Nate nodded sober agreement. Slade gazed thoughtfully into the valley for a moment, where four men were grouped around another on the ground, who was to all appearances dead. It being impossible to descend, he turned to see how his companions had fared in the rukus.

Nate Persinger was tying up a flesh wound in his left arm. Old Jethro swabbed the blood from a bullet gashed hand. Slade secured a jar of antiseptic ointment from his saddle pouch and smeared both wounds liberally and attended to his lightly creased jaw.

"Came out of it very well, all of us, which was more than I'd hoped for at first. By the way, did either of you ever see those hellions before?" Both men shook their heads.

"Strangers to the section so far as I can see," observed Jethro. "Mean looking cusses. Do you reckon the cattle fellers brought them here to do their shooting for them?"

"Not impossible, but highly unlikely, I'd say," Slade replied. "I'm of the opinion that the ranchers, especially Sid Claxton, whom I met last night and talked with, are not the sort to hire somebody to fight their battles."

"I can't help feel that maybe you're right," Jethro admitted. "They may be mean as a barrel of teased snakes, but somehow I can't see them doing a thing like that. But if they didn't bring 'em in, why did the skunks want to kill us farmers?"

"That's a question I'd like to have the answer to, but at present I haven't got it," Slade replied. "Let's see if we can find their cayuses—they should be around somewhere close and the brands might tell us something, although I doubt it."

They located the horses without difficulty, some distance along the cliff edge, tied in a thicket. All bore a Y Bench brand.

"That's an East Texas burn," Slade said. "Means nothing. Horses can be sold, traded or stolen, and jiggers like those back there usually ride horses bearing a faraway brand. I'll get the rigs off and turn them loose to fend for themselves until they're picked up; they'll make out all right. Notice one thing, and remember it: two of the rigs are new, the other three well-worn." The Persingers nodded and asked no questions.

"Reckon we'll have to report this to the sheriff when we get back to town," Jethro observed, adding, "but I figure it can wait till we pack the supplies to the boys at the flume. Besides, I want to ride back down the valley and learn who was killed, and how all this came to happen."

Slade nodded agreement, for he wished to get a look at the lake and its environs. With a last glance at the dead drygulchers they returned to their horses and continued the ride toward the head of the valley.

"Son, if I hadn't seen it I'd never have believed a feller could shoot a gun as fast as you did yours," Jethro suddenly remarked. "I figure you did for at least three of those skunks before me and Nate even got going. If we'd been alone we wouldn't have had a chance. Reckon what you told me the first time we met was gospel truth."

Not long afterward the trail veered away from the cliff head and ran for several miles almost due east. Then it turned north again and when the afternoon was well advanced, ran in the shadow of a mighty wall of stone which towered nearly a hundred feet into the air.

"That's what holds the lake back," said Jethro.

Slade gazed at the peculiar formation with the understanding eye of a geologist and his brows drew together in thought. The rock was black and striated. Moisture beaded its surface and here and there were little whorls and trickles of water seeping through the stone.

"Plutonie," Slade remarked. "It isn't overly thick, either."

"Thick enough, I reckon," returned Jethro. "We had quite a time of it busting through up to the top."

"Not overly thick when one considers the volume of water back of it," Slade answered. "There are millions of tons of water pressing against that wall of rock. Chances are it will hold, as it has done for a great many years. But if it happened to give, the water would sweep the valley from end to end, and everything alive with it."

"That's what I told you once, Dad," remarked Nate.

"Yes, reckon you did, but I figure she'll hold," Jethro replied complacently. "Around the bulge, now, and we'll see the flume."

Slade lingered a moment, studying the wall of rock. The trickles of water formed fantastic, ever-changing patterns on the dark stone. He experienced an uncanny feeling that those spirals and curlycues, the oozy squares and triangles, the melting rhomboids, the wavering tendrils and twirls were hieroglyphics of doom. As if an invisible hand were tracing a cryptic prophecy of disaster, of horror and death.

Nonsense! The wall had been there for hundreds of thousands, perhaps a million years, standing massive and firm. Doubtless so it would stand to the end of time unless some subterrestrial convulsion shook it down; and this was not an earthquake belt. Jethro Persinger was right, the wall would hold.

Thus reassuring himself, he tried to shake off the oppressive feeling; but it persisted. Oh, to the devil with it! The tragic happenings of the day had gotten on his nerves, that was all. With a shrug of his shoulders he turned his back on the ominous limnings that seemed to leer at him and followed Persinger around the bulge.

SIX

THE FLUME, BUILT OF DRESSED STONE, was from an engineer's viewpoint an admirable bit of work. Slade's respect for young Nate's ability rose still more. Without a doubt, the boy was a natural-born engineer, something not often encountered. He studied the flume and its construction and nodded approvingly. Running steeply from a gap in the lip of the wall, resting on arches of stone until it reached the sloping ground at the base of the wall, it continued on down the slope and out of sight in the growth.

Built where it could command the approach from all sides was a sturdy cabin. Slade sensed that eyes watched them from the narrow windows as they drew near. A moment later, however, a man with a rifle cradled in his arm stepped from the door and greeted the Persingers with a hail of recognition. He cast a questioning glance at Slade but soon was shaking his hand vigorously, as did a second man who had meanwhile appeared from the cabin, as old Jethro unfolded the story of what had happened on the cliff top farther south.

"Calc'late you to be a square man, even though you do look like a cattleman," one said in a nasal twang. "You always did know how to pick friends, Brother Persinger."

"Reckon he sort of picked me, Brother Bixby," Jethro replied with a dry chuckle. "It was a case of being picked or picked off, when first we met," he added with another chuckle at his own wit.

Slade and the Persingers ate with the flume guards and made preparations to spend the night in the shack.

"We got time, 'fore the sun goes down, to ride up the slope north of here and see the lake," Jethro said as they finished final cups of steaming coffee. "You of a mind to have a look at it, son?"

Slade signified his willingness and they set out, walking their horses up the steep slope.

The lake proved to be a vast sheet of water almost circular in shape. It lay some distance below the rim of the rock walls that enclosed it, devoid of motion, glassy as ice. The sun was low in the west and the great cup was filled with strange and mysterious fires.

It was a lonely scene, hauntingly beautiful. To the east the hills reared against the sky. To the west the ground sloped steeply down to the cliffs that bulwarked the valley, the wide depression of which could be seen from this height. Slade studied the motionless lake.

"This is nothing but an old volcanic crater or blowhole filled with water by subterranean springs, the residue of which drains off by some underground channel," was his verdict. "This whole section was highly volcanic thousands, maybe millions of years ago—there are signs of it everywhere. Over to the west not too many miles are the *Sierra de Cenizas*—the Ashes Mountains—which are almost pure lava. That's where, the story goes, Captain de Gavilan and his Spaniards got loads of nuggets and gold in the form of both wires and masses, although nobody else has ever been able to find their mines."

"Don't reckon there's any gold in these hills," remarked Jethro.

"I doubt it," Slade replied. "No indications of it so far as I can see. Also, the chances are this whole region has been thoroughly combed by prospectors.

"But there might be something else," he added thoughtfully, for that elusive chord of memory stirred as he regarded the peculiar formations. Stirred but refused to strike an explanatory note.

They got the details of the tragedy of the day before when they rode down to the valley the following morning.

"Poor Abner Price, the Sutton brothers, Sam Wheelock and Rias Richardson were crossing the meadow to the alfalfa field when those ornery tykes opened fire on them," their informant said. "Abner was shot dead, Cole Sutton got a busted arm, and Rias Richardson was shot through the shoulder. There was no place to hide or get under cover, so they just laid down in the grass and swapped lead with the cusses. They were in a bad way when all of a sudden they heard lots of shooting up top the cliffs and no more bullets came their direction. You and Nate and your friend did a mighty fine chore of work, Brother Persinger."

An inquest was held in Vereda two days later. Sheriff Crane Higgins, a stringy and cantankerous old frontier peace officer, pompously directed proceedings at the start. The coroner, white-haired and white-whiskered, looked bored until his keen and truculent eyes met Slade's. Then one lid dropped the merest trifle. Slade stifled a grin and nodded almost imperceptibly. The coroner, whom Slade knew well, was Doctor Austin, a Border country physician with a high reputation. He turned and banged his gavel.

"Sit down, Crane," he ordered the sheriff. "Too much ambling around in here." The sheriff looked indignant but subsided. He also looked as if he had something on his mind and was bursting to turn it loose. Slade, who had a pretty good notion what it was, bit back another grin with difficulty.

Most of the town was present, a number of the valley farmers, and many cattlemen from the ranches to the north and east, the story of the drygulching having spread like wildfire. Sam Wheelock and the unwounded Sutton brother told their story of the treacherous attack. They were followed by Jethro Persinger and his son Nate, who detailed what happened on the cliff top. Then Walt Slade was called to the stand. After several formal questions by the coroner, he repeated the story as told by the Persingers.

Sheriff Higgins could evidently contain himself no longer. He heaved his stringy form from his chair and bent a not very friendly stare on Slade's face.

"Name's Slade, eh?" he rumbled. "Ever been called something else? Ever been called El Halcon, Mexican talk for The Hawk?"

Slade met the sheriff's accusing stare with faintly amused eyes. "Uh-huh, been called that," he admitted, apparently oblivious to the sensation the sheriff's question had created.

"I've heard tell of you!" barked the sheriff. "I've heard you've been mixed up in a deal of killings all over Texas."

Slade's lips quirked at the corners. "Ever hear of me killing anybody who didn't have a killing coming?" he asked mildly in his musical voice.

Sheriff Higgins flushed at the implied reproof. "That's beside the point," he replied. "Enforcing the law is to be left to duly elected or appointed peace officers. Folks aren't supposed to take the law into their own hands, like I've heard you do. What happened the other day is an example of what I'm talking about."

The quirking of Slade's lips widened to a smile that flashed his even teeth startlingly white in his bronzed face.

"Sorry, Sheriff," he chuckled, "but there just naturally wasn't time to hustle to town and tell you what was going on. I was afraid those hellions wouldn't wait to pull trigger till after I got back with you."

Chuckles interspersed by hearty guffaws ruffled the dignity of the coroner's court. Doc Austin, however, looked amused and refrained from banging his gavel. The sheriff's mustache bristled in his scarlet face.

"I've a notion to lock you up!" he roared.

The smile left Slade's lips, and his eyes were abruptly cold as the shadowy waters of the lake in the hills above the valley.

"What for?" he asked in soft tones that nevertheless sobered every man in the courtroom.

The sheriff flushed even more darkly under the contempt in Slade's steady gaze. He was about to return a furious reply when a precise, modulated voice broke in. It was the voice of Rex Masters, Blaine Webb's partner in the Diamond Flush saloon and the Diamond W ranch, who was foreman of the jury—

"As I understand it, we are here to fix the responsibility for the death of six men, and to advise punishment, if any, for those responsible for the deaths. I would suggest that we attend to the business at hand before going into extraneous matters."

Doc Austin's gavel hit the table with a blacksmith's blow. "Shut up, Crane," he told the sheriff. "Masters is right."

The sheriff snorted and rumbled, and subsided again. Quite likely he welcomed the interruption which gave him an out from a situation in which he was beginning to look ridiculous. But the baleful glare he bent on Slade said plainer than words that he was itching for a chance to even the score. Doc Austin requested a verdict from the jury.

The verdict was short, to the point, and typical cow country—Abner Price was murdered, which shouldn't have happened to him even if he was a nester, by five hellions who got what was coming to them. Slade and the Persingers did a good chore.

All eyes followed The Hawk's tall form as he left the courtroom, the man whose questionable exploits were legendary throughout the Southwest, and discussed with much difference of opinion wherever peace officers or Texas fighting men got together, of whom it was said by many—"If he ain't an owlhoot, he misses being one by the skin of his teeth!"

Violent arguments broke out as soon as he had departed. However, the general agreement was with the jury's verdict—that Slade had done a good chore on the cliff top.

Before Slade had gone far, old Jethro and Nate caught up with him.

"I've heard tell of El Halcon, too," said Jethro. "Reckon most everybody hereabouts has. But nobody's going to convince us farmers that you ain't a square man who does the right thing. You're welcome at my farmhouse, son, and any other farmhouse in the valley, whenever you're of a mind to pay a visit."

Slade smiled down at the old man from his great height, and his normally cold eyes were warm and sunny.

"Thank you," he said simply. "I'll be there soon as I get the chance."

Sid Claxton was sitting at a table when Slade entered the Diamond Flush, a little later. He beckoned El Halcon to join him. After Slade sat down and drinks had been ordered, Claxton regarded his table companion seriously.

"Son," he said, "I'd like to ask you a straight question, and I'd like a straight answer."

"Shoot!" Slade replied, smiling. Claxton leaned forward.

"Did the farmers bring you here to do their gun slinging for them?"

"They did not," Slade answered.

Claxton drew back and nodded. "That's enough for me," he said. "If you say they didn't, they didn't."

"And now, Mr. Claxton, I'd like to ask you a question," Slade countered. "And I think I'm entitled to a straight answer. Have the cowmen been bringing in paid killers to do their fighting for them?"

"Heck, no!" growled Claxton. "We're plumb capable of doing our own fighting when fighting becomes necessary."

"Well," Slade said, "somebody has been."

"What makes you say that, son?" Claxton asked.

"You'll recall, sir, that nobody was able to recognize those five killers," Slade pointed out. "Nobody who viewed the bodies could recall ever seeing them before. Three of those men were renegade cowhands who had not worked at their trade for a long time. The other two were gamblers dressed as cowhands, in new clothes. They had all the marks of the gambling fraternity, including sandpapered fingertips. Why should such a queer combination have any personal reason for killing the farmers?"

Claxton looked bewildered. "Have to admit it don't seem to make sense," he conceded.

"It certainly doesn't," Slade said. "And by the way, despite the fact that you appear to have no use for them, do the farmers strike you as the kind of men who would bring in killers, even if they had the money to pay them, which they haven't?"

This time old Sid looked uncomfortable under Slade's steady gaze; his eyes wandered about the room and he flushed slightly.

"No, blast their ornery hides! they don't," he finally exploded, giving Slade an injured glare. "Darn you, you get me all mixed up!"

Slade's eyes danced. "It may help you to get unscrambled, later," he said.

Old Sid threw out his hands in despair. "Half the time I don't know what the blankety-blank-blank you're talking about, but it bothers me!" he wailed. "Thank Pete here comes Verna! She'll be a match for you. Sit down, chick, and take over this young hellion. He's got my twine tangled. I'm going over to the bar and have a dozen drinks to take the knots out!"

Slade rose to his feet and pulled out the vacant chair for Verna to occupy. The red-haired girl dropped into it, and for some reason known to herself, blushed hotly under his regard.

"You certainly have a pretty color today," he remarked innocently, but with laughter in his eyes.

"What woman wouldn't have—under the circumstances!" she retorted. "But what did you do to Dad? The poor old dear is all confused."

"I hope I started him thinking a little," Slade replied, suddenly serious.

"He seems very disturbed."

"Thought can often be disturbing, but also often productive of good."

She shook her bright head. "You're a strange man, Walt," she said. "You seem to have the ability to make anyone do what you want them to do."

"Perhaps," he smiled, "I just help them to do what they've been wanting to do all along, even if they didn't realize it."

Verna blushed again. "You may have the right idea there," she conceded, the dimple showing at the corner of her mouth, enhancing, Slade thought, its scarlet witchery. "I hope Dad will be as easy to convince as I—" She left the sentence unfinished and the glow of her cheeks deepened still more. "I hope so; for I'm sure anything you persuade him to do will be for his own good."

"Like yourself?"

"Yes, darn it! and you know it!"

"I'm optimistic about him," Slade said, and meant it. He felt that he had sowed certain seeds of doubt in the old shorthorn's mind and was content to give them a chance to grow.

"I think that inside, well covered up, he is a kindly sympathetic person, although he refuses to admit it— yet," he continued. "Just give him time."

"He is," Verna said. "I've seen tears in his eyes when he worked over a sick calf, and he's helped people who never knew from where the help came. He's quick-tempered and, to use an expression, 'sot in his ways,' but a more honest man never lived. What he believes, he believes, but he can change his mind, under a little gentle persuasion."

"Such as twisting his ear?" Slade smiled.

"Oh, I can always handle him, to a certain extent," she replied. "But changing an opinion he has once formed is not easy, even for me. He'll merely laugh at me and say women don't understand such things. I hope you don't agree with him on that score."

"If there's anything they don't understand, I've still to find it out," Slade said with conviction. "Perhaps when I'm as old as your Dad I'll know more about it."

"You won't," she said flatly.

As they talked, Slade's keen ears caught snatches of conversation. The cattlemen appeared uncertain as to the reason for the drygulching. Some voiced the opinion that it might have been a personal matter on the part of men whose enmity had been aroused by questionable acts on the part of the nesters in some other locality. These, however, were in the minority, he gathered. For the most part the ranchers seemed quite puzzled.

Sid Claxton, staring moodily into his glass, took no part in the discussion, and men, after a glance at him, left him alone.

"He's all set to blow sky high over something," Slade heard one oldtimer mutter to another. "Don't know what's come over him; he 'pears all bothered about something."

Which caused the Ranger to stifle a grin.

"You're not paying any attention to me!" Verna exclaimed petulantly.

"Sorry," he apologized. "I was listening to the chatter."

"I was, too," she admitted; "I find it interesting. I never heard them talk like this before. They seem doubtful about things, really concerned by that farmer's death." Slade nodded agreement.

One man, a stringy individual with a furtive manner, apparently did not read old Sid's mood aright or chose to ignore it; he sidled up to him insinuatingly, spoke a few words.

"What!" roared Claxton. "You talk like a blasted fool! Of course I'm not glad the nester got killed! Get away from me, you mangy horned toad!"

Under his glare, the man scuttled off like a scared rat.

"That was Pete Houck, who rides for the Diamond W," Verna remarked. "I don't think Dad likes him."

"An outstanding example of understatement, I'd say," Slade replied dryly. The red-haired girl looked very thoughtful.

"The Diamond W, that's the spread owned by Masters and Webb, is it not?" he added.

"Yes," she said, "the ranch this side of ours, next to the hills. It's a very good holding with more water than most. Being so close to the hills is an advantage. Quite a few springs flow trickles onto their land."

"Do they own the hills?"

Verna shook her head. "No, the hills are included in the land the farmers bought," she explained. "They were part of the State land which extended on through the hills to the west of the valley and were included in the purchase. Not good for much, I suppose, judging from what Dad and others say." It was Slade's turn to look thoughtful.

"I can't get over the way Dad chased Pete Houck," she resumed. "He acted as if he were downright insulted by whatever Pete said to him."

Her expressive eyes darkened, seemed to gaze into the future.

"I think," she said slowly, "that perhaps that poor farmer did not die in vain."

"In the long ago, a Man died on a Cross of agony, and not in vain," Slade replied gently. Verna bowed her head.

SEVEN

Suddenly old Sid whirled from the bar and lumbered over to the table.

"Let's get the heck out of here and ride for the spread," he growled. "I'm sick and tired of this gabfest. Come along with us, Slade."

"Be glad to," the Ranger replied as Verna's eyes seconded the invitation.

They had ridden for some distance, in silence, when old Sid said gruffly,

"Slade, do something for me, will you? Find out if that nester who was killed left a wife and kids."

"I certainly will, Mr. Claxton," Slade replied, glancing at Verna, who bit back a smile.

Slade was impressed by the excellence of the range and said so.

"Yes," said Claxton, "it's fine cattle land, and we're trying to keep it that way." His face darkened. "We would, too, easy, if it wasn't for those pests over there," jerking his thumb toward Vereda Valley.

"They're not good neighbors?" Slade asked.

"Oh, I ain't got anything against them as neighbors," Claxton replied. "They tend to their own business, keep to themselves, and don't bother other folks. But they're just like grasshoppers—once they start coming there's no stopping them."

Slade asked another question, "Mr. Claxton, is the valley, now that it's irrigated, valuable enough to the cowmen to start a range war over?"

"Heck, no!" Claxton answered. "It's no good for cows, no matter how much water's in it; too hard to work. And we've got plenty of land over here. But here's the trouble, son. Let me tell you about something that happened over to the east of here quite a ways. That was first-rate cow country. Folks were getting along fine, but there was a

46

lot of land there that was open range, claimed by the State. I ain't going to argue the legality of open range, no matter what my private opinion is. The fact remains that the courts have consistently ruled in favor of the State. Well, over there a big Eastern syndicate bought up all the open range, and bought a couple of spreads from fellers willing to sell. Then they began running nesters in, although I reckon that really ain't the right word for them no more than for those cusses in the valley; they bought their land from the syndicate and paid for it. But they ran fences, shut in the waterholes and the springs. Soon the cowland wasn't any good as cowland— you can't raise cows without water. The nesters took over; now they own the whole section and it's all fenced. See?

"We've got good cowland here, although we could do with a mite more water. Got enough to get by with, though, so long as none is fenced in. I own my land, every acre of it, but over beyond my holding there's a lot of open range. Now if that was bought up like it was over to the east and sold to the nesters, look what would happen here. That's what we're trying to prevent. The bunch in the valley are an opening wedge and we know it, that's why we don't want 'em here. I ain't saying anything, right now, about poisoned waterholes and wide-looped cows. If they're responsible for those things, sooner or later we'll catch 'em at it. That sort of thing you can fight, but not what I've just been telling you about."

"Why don't the owners to the east of your holding acquire the open range land by purchase from the State?" Slade asked. "Looks like to me that would go a long ways toward solving your problem."

Claxton shrugged. "Mostly oldtimers over there, most of 'em even older than me, and sot in their ways. They say they own that land by right of occupancy over a long period of years, their fathers and grandfathers before them, and that they'll fight to hold it, come hell, high water and nesters."

"And lose," Slade said positively. "That is, if it comes to a showdown with the State. But in my opinion you'll never have to face that problem. This land is not good

farming land and the farmers know it. That's why they
bought in Vereda Valley instead of over there to the east.
You can't irrigate this land, and without irrigation it
would not be productive enough so far as crops are concerned to pay off. Only because young Nate Persinger
has the makings of a fine engineer did they occupy Vereda
Valley, which formerly was also no good for farming."

"You may be right," Claxton admitted, "but," he added
obstinately, "the fact remains that till the farmers showed
up we hadn't had any trouble worth mentioning hereabouts for years."

Slade noted his use for the first time of the word
"farmers" to designate the valley dwellers and smiled
slightly but did not comment. They rode on.

"There's the Diamond W casa," Claxton remarked a
little later, jerking his thumb at a ranchhouse a little distance from the trail. It was not very large but in excellent repair, as were the bunkhouse, barn and other
buildings.

"Webb and Masters are bachelors and don't need much
room but they sure keep their little shack in tiptop shape,"
Claxton commented. Slade nodded agreement.

"That blasted drygulching," old Sid suddenly said in
querulous tones, "it just doesn't seem to make sense."

"Mr. Claxton," Slade replied, "you'll recall that all five
of those sidewinders wore rangeland clothes, although two
of the outfits were new and worn by men who were obviously not range riders. Suppose you were a farmer and
saw those men in cowhand garb riding away from the
scene, after the shooting, what would you have thought."

"Well," old Sid admitted reluctantly, "I reckon I'd have
figured they were some riders from this section."

"And that is exactly what would have happened had
it not been for the fortunate accident of the Persingers
and myself arriving on the scene when we did and making
it possible for all to see that those five men were strangers
to the section. That is what was intended to happen. The
result might well have been serious trouble between the
farmers, who are not the sort to be pushed around with
impunity, and the cattlemen who, knowing they were

not responsible for what happened, would have defended their position vigorously."

"But who in blazes was responsible, and why?" demanded Claxton, looking baffled. "It still don't seem to make sense."

"I don't know the answer to either question, but I hope to learn them," Slade said grimly. Old Sid glanced at his set face and icy eyes and refrained from asking questions. Verna smiled.

All in all, Slade was as puzzled as old Sid. The whole affair really did not seem to make sense. The valley, while productive, was certainly not a bonanza in any sense of the word. It would afford a living for its dwellers, with plenty of hard work, but that was all. He was becoming of the opinion that somebody was deliberately endeavoring to stir up trouble with the object of driving the farmers from their holdings; but why? What was to be gained by so doing? Nothing, so far as he could see. There was certainly neither gold nor silver in the hills. Some other mineral of worth? What? Oil? As an engineer and geologist he knew very well there was not. No salt domes, no salt springs; nothing to point toward petroleum pools beneath the valley. Copper? He shook his head; not in these volcanic hills.

An insidious doubt began crawling in the back of his mind. Perhaps he was wrong in his estimate of the cattlemen. He had not met them all. He could very well be making a grave mistake. He recalled the malicious lear on Pete Houck's face as he sidled up to old Sid. Sometimes riders got out of hand and did things their employers would not countenance. Some men seemed to have a streak of pure devilishness in them and experienced a sadistic pleasure from inflicting pain and trouble on others. And he well knew that there was such a thing as a born killer, the type that joyed in killing for its own sake.

The farmers? Well, he hadn't met all of them either. Those he had met made a good impression on him, but there's usually a rotten apple in every barrel. His judgment of all and sundry must be held in abeyance until he was in a better position to consider all the angles. However, Captain Jim had sent him into the section with a definite chore to do, and he intended to do it.

Returning to the farmers—some of them, feeling that they were being unjustly imposed upon and bitterly resenting the cattleman's overbearing attitude, might be out to even the score. Outnumbered, they could not hope to carry direct conflict to the ranchers and would resort to devious means of retaliation. On both sides a war of nerves with tension mounting until some overt act might bring about explosive violence. For there was no doubt but that each faction still regarded the other with suspicion.

He took some small comfort from the changing attitude of Sid Claxton who was evidently a power among the ranchers. Unless all signs failed, the Cross C owner was not as positive of the justification of his attitude as he had been. An element of doubt had intruded, Slade believed. And perhaps certain qualms of conscience were making themselves felt. If so, his task might well be simplified, so far as preventing serious trouble was concerned. Where Claxton led, the ranchers, a majority of them at least, would follow. He'd keep on prodding the old shorthorn and perhaps some development might tend to strengthen the influence he believed he was getting over him.

A development was due to take place in short order, but not one wholly to the Ranger's liking.

"There she is!" old Sid suddenly exclaimed, pointing to a big white ranchhouse set well back from the trail and shaded by ancient oaks. "Nice, don't you think?"

"Yes, very nice," Slade said. "It would appear life has been good to you, Mr. Claxton."

"Oh, I can't complain," old Sid conceded complacently.

"Yes, very good," Slade repeated, "much more so than to many who are glad to have a roof of any kind over their heads, and enough to eat—sometimes, but who nevertheless humbly give thanks for what they do have."

"Just what do you mean by that?" Claxton asked slowly.

"On my way to Vereda I stopped and ate at a house

over in the valley," Slade answered, his gaze on the commodious Cross C casa. "It was a small house, not much
more than a cabin, and roughly built by the hands of two
men, an old one and a young one. We ate in the kitchen,
for there was no dining room, a very simple meal, but
thanks were given for the food we were about to consume
before we partook of it."

Slade turned his head and let the full force of his steady
gray eyes rest on the other's face. For a moment old Sid
met the gaze of those pale, cold eyes that abruptly were
filled with compassion. Then he turned away and his
face flushed darkly. His usually forceful voice was strangely
lifeless when he spoke.

"The boys will take care of the horses," he said. "Come
on in."

Slade okayed a wrangler for Shadow and the big black
was led away. He followed old Sid up the wide veranda
steps. Verna dropped back beside him, and there were
tears in her eyes.

"He's not accustomed to having somebody feel sorry
for him," she whispered. "You do feel sorry for him,
don't you? I read it in your face."

"Yes," Slade said gently. "I do."

The big living room of the casa was tastefully and lav-
ishly furnished. Included was a grand piano. Old Sid
glanced at it. "She's a good one," he said. "Do you happen
to play the piano, too?" Slade nodded.

"Then maybe you'll sing for us this evening," Claxton
insinuated.

"I'll be glad to, if you really wish it," Slade replied.

"Oh, please do!" Verna begged.

"Show him the place, chick," Claxton said. He opened
a door.

"Here's the—dining room," he said. "We need a big
one with the hands we got," he added, almost apolo-
getically. "That door across the room leads to the kitchen.
That's where Verna hangs out a lot. Oh, she can cook,
and do housework. She'll make some jigger a good wife
someday. That is if he's lucky enough to—have a house."

"If he hasn't, perhaps he'll build one," Slade said smilingly. Old Sid grunted, and looked away.

"Take him upstairs," he said to Verna. "Give him the big room, the second one from the stairhead. I'm going out and tell the cook to rustle his hocks; I'm hungry."

The house was built in the Spanish style, with balconies and an inner patio. It was supplied with running water, there being a big tank on the roof which was fed by a ram that drew it from a spring at the base of the rise. Altogether a very comfortable, even luxurious establishment.

Verna led the way up the stairs and opened the first door. "Mine," she said, revealing a chamber that was daintily feminine. Another door, two down the hall, was commodious and well furnished. The windows were floor length.

"All the windows open onto the balcony," Verna said, with a giggle. "It's nice out there at night."

"Yes?" Slade smiled. Verna blushed.

"Dad sleeps at the far end of the hall," she said. "Clem Yates, the range boss, across the hall from him. There are two more guest chambers."

EIGHT

SLADE SPENT A VERY ENJOYABLE NIGHT and morning at the Cross C ranchhouse. He met the hands and liked them. In the afternoon Claxton announced his intention to ride to town to transact some business. Despite Verna's protest, Slade decided to ride with him. He wanted to get, if possible, the particulars concerning the dependents, if any, of Abner Price, the murdered farmer.

As luck would have it, he contacted Jethro Persinger soon after arriving at Vereda.

"A young wife and three younkers," Persinger replied in answer to his question. "Reckon it'll go sort of hard with them this winter, but us fellers will do all we can."

Slade asked another question. "Well," Jethro answered, "the boys are sort of divided as to who was responsible for the killing. Some feel that somehow the cattle fellers were back of it. Others ain't sure. I passed on the word that you were sure Claxton and his bunch had nothing to do with it, and that packed considerable weight, but some of the boys keep asking if it wasn't the cattlemen, who was it? Nobody 'pears to have an answer for that one."

"I haven't myself," Slade admitted. "However, I hope to have before the last brand is run."

"I've a notion you'll get it," Jethro said. "Yep, I'm plumb certain you will, only I hope it ain't too late. Bad trouble could bust loose any time."

With which Slade was heartily in agreement. He spent the rest of the afternoon and the early evening moseying about the town, listening to conversations in the various places where men gathered, studying faces, and learned nothing that he considered of importance.

Late in the evening he repaired to the Diamond Flush for his dinner. Blaine Webb was not in evidence and Rex Masters appeared to be in charge. He sauntered over and joined Slade while he was waiting for his order to be prepared.

"Yes, Webb is taking the night off," he replied to a remark by the Ranger. "We were both busy at the ranch today and he was tired, so I volunteered to take over tonight.

"It would seem you have been quite active since you arrived here, Mr. Slade," he observed pleasantly. "Incidentally, I thought the way you handled Sheriff Higgins at the inquest quite amusing."

"The sheriff's all right," Slade said. "Sort of cantankerous and gets his bristles up easily, but okay."

"He's vindictive," Masters said. "He'll make trouble for you if he gets the opportunity."

"If he gets the opportunity," Slade smiled. Masters shot him a quick look but did not comment.

"Hope you'll see fit to stay with us," he said. "We need men like—"

"El Halcon?" Slade finished smilingly. Masters shrugged his shoulders, which were broad for so slender a man.

"I can't say as I take much stock in the El Halcon stories," he said. "Very likely they are highly exaggerated."

"Possibly," Slade agreed. Masters laughed and returned to the bar, which was busy.

After eating and smoking a cigarette, Slade paused at the bar for a drink and a chance to study the room in the back bar mirror. A little later Sid Claxton entered and paused beside the Ranger.

"Going to have one snort and then hit the hay," he said. "Don't feel like riding back to the spread tonight. Would have to come in tomorrow, for I didn't finish all I had planned. Got me a room upstairs."

"I think I'll call it a day myself before long," Slade replied.

Claxton nodded and tossed off his drink. "By the way, did you learn anything about that farmer who was killed?"

Slade relayed the information he had gathered from Jethro Persinger. Claxton nodded thoughtfully. "See you in the morning," he said and departed. A few moments later, Slade also left the saloon and climbed the outer stairs to his room. He was just passing the door at the head of the stairs, which stood partly open, when from inside the room came the muffled boom of a shot, followed by a thud. He whirled and shoved the door wide open, slewing sideways as he did so.

A lance of flame gushed from the darkness. Lead screeched through the opening, fanning his face with its lethal breath. He jerked his guns and fired at the flash. There was a crash of broken glass and another thud, outside the room. Slade leaped toward the shattered window, weaving and ducking, tripped over something and fell headlong. Instinctively he rolled aside, throwing down with the one gun that remained in his hand in the direction of the object on the floor. It did not move. He picked up his fallen gun, scrambled to his feet and stuck his head through the smashed window. The building wall fronted on a dark and narrow side street; there was nobody in sight.

Light streaming in from the hall showed a body on the floor. He bent over it and started back in horror. He was gazing into the blood streaked face of Sid Claxton.

NINE

OUTSIDE, SHOUTS WERE SOUNDING, and feet pounding on the stairs. Slade straightened up, holstered his guns, fumbled a match and struck it. He touched the flame to the wick of a bracket lamp and turned to the door as a soft glow filled the room.

Men were streaming through the doorway. In the forefront was Sheriff Crane Higgins. He held a gun which he trained on the Ranger.

"So!" he rumbled exultantly. "Tangled your twine at last, eh! Face the wall with your hands against it."

Slade obeyed; there was nothing else to do. Half a dozen guns were menacing him. His Colts were plucked from their sheaths. The sheriff reamed a fingertip in the barrel of one.

"Been fired plumb recent!" he crowed. "We'll see if you can slide from under a murder charge!"

Slade sighed. Looked like the finish of El Halcon in the section, which he didn't wish to happen. The sheriff was chortling with delight.

Suddenly a diversion occurred. Behind them was a groan and a feeble oath. All eyes slanted in the direction of the sound. The "dead" man was sitting up, pawing at his bloody forehead. With returning strength he glared about, swore explosively.

"What the devil's going on here?" he demanded. "Why are you hellions holding guns on Slade?"

The sheriff gawked and goggled like a newly landed fish. "D-didn't he shoot you?" he stuttered.

"Of course he didn't shoot me, you ganglin' terrapin-brain!" bawled old Sid, lurching to his feet to stand weaving and mopping his face with a handkerchief. "Why the devil should he shoot me? I left him in the bar when I headed for bed. I stopped at the foot of the stairs to talk with Jim Underwood a minute and when I came up and opened my door, some blankety-blank-blank son of a skunk holed up in the room let me have it. Have you all gone loco?"

The sheriff gave a despairing groan and glowered at Slade. "Can't nobody ever get anything on you!" he lamented, shoving the Ranger's guns back to him. "Well, what did you see? No matter what else you are, I don't figure you for a liar. What did you see?"

"Not much," Slade replied. "I heard the shot as I was passing, shoved the door open and came close to eating lead myself; you'll find a bullet hole in the wall out there opposite the door. I blasted a couple of shots at the hellion, but he went through the window. I'm afraid I missed him in my flurry. You might look around outside, though, to make sure."

"Yes, and the whole crowd of you get out of here!" shouted Claxton. "I'm all right; Slade will look after me. And don't come back," he added as the crowd, looking sheepish, followed the disgruntled sheriff. Slade shut the door and turned to the rancher.

"And now suppose you sit down and let me have a look at your head," he suggested.

Old Sid obeyed and Slade examined the bullet cut just in front of his left temple at the hairline. He probed the wound with gentle, sensitive fingers.

"Don't think it amounts to much," was his verdict. "Wait, I have a bandage and antiseptic ointment in my room." He hurried out and returned quickly with the medicants. Soon the wound, which had practically ceased to bleed, was smeared with the ointment and bandaged.

"But it might be a good notion to have Doctor Austin look at it, too," he said. "Never can tell for sure about a hard blow like that; there's such a thing as concussion, you know."

Old Sid was looking up at him, a strange expression on

his lined face. "Hit me a hefty wallop, all right," he said. "Son, I'm pretty sure you saved my life. When that slug creased me and knocked me down, it sort of paralyzed me—I couldn't move a finger—but I didn't lose my senses for a minute, and I saw the hellion bending over me with a knife in his hand; he was going to use it. If you hadn't barged in when you did he would have slit my throat."

"Did you get a look at his face?" Slade asked.

"Not much of a one," Claxton replied. "It was sort of long and white and lean. I'm sure, though, that I never saw him before. Wonder if it was somebody from over in the valley? What are you looking for, son?"

"The slug that creased you," Slade replied. "It could be in here somewhere. Yes, there it is, stuck in the door jamb."

With his knife he carefully removed the bullet. The nose was slightly flattened but it was otherwise intact. Slade turned it over in his slender fingers.

"Heft it," he said, passing it to Claxton, who did so, bouncing it on his palm.

"Feels sort of light," the rancher said.

"It is," Slade replied; "too light for a Forty-five. The fact that it isn't a Forty-five very likely kept you from being killed. You've evidently got a hard head and the slug glanced off. A Forty-five fired from a long barreled gun would have gone straight through, and it would have pierced the door jamb for a couple of inches, at least, instead of sticking in the surface. I'd say the caliber is Forty-one, and it was fired from a gun with a very short barrel. Very likely a double-barreled derringer, a sleeve gun, the gambler's gun it's called. Fits into a sleeve holster and can be slid into the palm by a jerk of the wrist."

"Darned if I don't figure you're right," said Claxton.

"And, Mr. Claxton," Slade pursued, "did you ever hear of a farmer packing a sleeve gun?" Old Sid shook his head.

"And I doubt if you ever will," Slade continued. "All in all, I think we can eliminate the farmers as suspects."

"I figure you're right," Claxton repeated, "but if not one of them, who?"

"I don't know," Slade admitted frankly. "Can you think

of somebody who might be on the prod against you, holding a grudge because of something that happened?"

Claxton slowly shook his head. "I've had rows with fellers, but I'm darned if I can see any of 'em taking that kind of a shot at me. Listen! Somebody's coming up the stairs; get your gun ready."

Slade didn't think it necessary and opened the door in answer to a knock to admit Sheriff Crane Higgins. Claxton favored him with a not overly friendly look.

"Now what?" he growled.

"We went over every foot of the ground outside and didn't find anybody," the sheriff said to Slade. "But I got a lantern and found a few bloodspots.

"Looked like you might have winged the sidewinder."

"Possibly," Slade conceded, "but he could hardly have gone through the window the way he did without cutting himself."

"It's a wonder he didn't bust his neck," grunted the sheriff.

"I expect he was a fairly small man, very light on his feet," Slade said. "He sure went through that window like a cat with its tail afire. I imagine he lit running. You might keep your eyes open for a gent of that sort with a few scratches."

"If I get my paws on him he'll have scratches," the sheriff predicted darkly. "How do you feel, Sid?"

"I feel like having a drink," replied Claxton. "What say, Slade, suppose we go downstairs and get one; all the sleep's knocked out of me for a while."

"A good notion," Slade agreed; "I feel the same way. Have one with us, Sheriff?"

"Reckon I could do worse," replied the peace officer.

There were stares aplenty when the three entered the Diamond Flush together. The urbane Rex Masters came hurrying over to solicitiously ask Claxton how he felt.

"I'd feel a blasted sight worse if it wasn't for Slade here," old Sid boomed in a voice that resounded throughout the room. "He kept me from getting my comeuppance."

"Mr. Slade, the community owes you a vote of thanks,"

said Masters. "Mr. Claxton would have been an irreparable loss."

"Thank you, Mr. Masters," Slade replied.

Masters nodded and escorted them to the bar. "On the house, the best," he told the drink juggler.

Other men came to congratulate Claxton on his escape and to compliment Slade. Sheriff Higgins tugged his mustache.

"Reckon that goes for me, too," he said gruffly. "You did a fine chore, son."

"Thank you, Sheriff," Slade said, his eyes dancing. "Coming from you, that means a great deal to me."

The sheriff scowled ferociously to hide his evident embarrassment. "But you watch your step," he warned. "I don't want a lot of promiscuous killings in my bailiwick."

"Crane," said old Sid, "sometime I'm going to tie you in a double bowknot and hang you on a barbed wire fence. Have another drink."

Claxton had several after the sheriff departed. "Feeling a darn sight better," he declared. "Head don't ache any more. How are you?"

"Fine," Slade assured him. "If you feel up to it, suppose we walk over and have Doc Austin take a look at your head? Just a precaution. I suppose you know where his office is?"

"Sure, it ain't far," replied Claxton. "Okay, I'm ready if you are. Might be a good notion. As you said, you can't always tell about a whack on the head. Sometimes causes trouble later. Let's go." He waved goodnight to Masters, who bowed and smiled and watched them pass through the swinging doors, his pale eyes inscrutable.

They found the doctor in his office, reading. "Now what?" he asked, closing his book and frowning at Claxton.

Old Sid told him, stressing the part Slade played in the affair. The doctor nodded, not appearing particularly surprised.

"All right," he said. "Come on in back and I'll look you over. You did a good chore of bandaging, son; you can wait here."

He escorted Claxton to the rear of the building, but a few minutes later returned to Slade.

"How's McNelty?" he whispered.

"Fine as frog hair," Slade replied. "I'll tell him I saw you. How long you been here, Doc?"

"About a year—too long," the physician answered. "Was figuring to pull out soon. I'll stick around a while now that you're here, though; business is due to pick up. Drop in and see me when you get a chance. May have something to tell you." With a grin, he returned to his patient.

A little later old Sid appeared, wearing a fresh bandage. "Nothing to it," the doctor said. "You couldn't dent his skull with a sledge hammer. Put him to bed to sleep it off."

"Just a minute," Slade said. "Doctor, would you please weigh this slug and give me the weight in grains?"

Austin procured his delicate scales and quickly gave the weight. Slade nodded with satisfaction.

"Just as I figured, a Forty-one," he said to Claxton. "Thank you, Doctor."

On the way back to their rooms, Claxton said, "Meet me in the Diamond Flush about noon tomorrow, will you? Important."

Slade promised to do so and they went to bed. Slade did not immediately go to sleep, however. For some time he lay reviewing the recent hectic events and endeavoring to analyze them. Although still thoroughly puzzled by the situation, he felt there was one angle of satisfaction to be gleaned from them. He had undoubtedly greatly strengthened his influence over Sid Claxton, which he deemed highly important.

But, he was forced to morosely admit, that was about all. So far there was no explanation of the happenings other than a feud between the farmers and the cattlemen, with each faction striking subtly and vaguely at the other. It was too darned obvious, and Slade had learned to distrust the obvious.

Of course, despite his insistence to the contrary, the attack on Claxton might well have been motivated by a personal grudge. Arrogant, high-handed and domineering, he could have made enemies more bitter than he thought. Such men, positive in their belief in themselves and in the validity of their acts, callously brushing all opposition aside, sometimes inflicted wounds deeper than they realized. What seemed to them but an incident could be to the recipient grim tragedy and a great wrong. A spell of brooding over an injustice, real or fancied, sometimes resulted in explosive action.

The same line of reasoning could apply to the farmers. Again the obvious, and too coincidental. He muttered disgustedly, turned over and went to sleep.

TEN

SLADE MET SID CLAXTON in the Diamond Flush at noon the next day. The rancher passed him a tightly wrapped and tied flat packet.

"Think you could get it to the widow of that farmer?" he asked.

"I'm sure I can," Slade replied.

"Okay, get it to her," Claxton said gruffly. "And listen, I don't want anybody to know where it came from. Promise?"

"I promise," Slade answered, smiling broadly. Old Sid snorted and ordered a drink. A little later he said,

"The boys are going to hold a little meeting at my place tomorrow night. Think you could be there?"

"Don't see any reason why I can't," Slade replied.

"Fine!" said Claxton; "I'll be looking for you. We'll expect you to spend the night, and maybe we can ride over the spread the next day. I'd like you to see my holding, then maybe I can argue you into signing up with me."

"I'll be there," Slade assured him. "I'm going to ride up the valley after a bit and see to it that your package is delivered without delay. Also, I want to have a close look at those eastern cliffs that wall the valley."

"A look at the cliffs?" old Sid repeated in his booming voice. "What's interesting about those rocks?"

"Hard to tell," Slade answered. "They're a peculiar formation. I'll see you tomorrow evening."

"Okay," nodded Claxton. "I'm heading back to the spread now; got all my business transacted," he added with elaborate carelessness.

Slade had trouble keeping from smiling; he had a very good notion as to what the "business" was Claxton had been so anxious to transact. He waved to Rex Masters, who evidently frequented the saloon in the daytime. Masters smiled and waved back. A little later he got the rig on Shadow and rode up Vereda Valley, headed for Jethro Persinger's holding.

He didn't know it, but keen eyes watched him ride out of town and noted the direction he turned. A very few minutes later, two men also rode out of town, their saddle pouches well plumped out. They did not turn into Vereda Valley, however, but skirted the hills and rode north at a fast pace, toward where the old trail wound up the slopes and eventually reached the lip of the cliff wall which bulwarked the valley.

When Slade arrived at the farmhouse he found the Persingers pottering about their garden patch and received a warm welcome.

"Come on in for coffee and a snack," invited Jethro. "We were just thinking of knocking off for a spell. Things are growing fine."

As they sat at table, Slade produced the packet given him by Sid Claxton and handed it to Jethro.

"See that Abner Price's widow gets it," he requested. "And I'd suggest that you take care of it; I've a notion it's valuable."

Persinger eyed the packet curiously. "Where'd it come from?" he asked.

"From somebody who sympathizes with her bereavement," Slade replied. "No, not from myself."

Jethro still looked curious but refrained from asking questions.

"Where you headed for, son?" he asked as Slade drained a final cup of steaming coffee and stood up.

"I'm going to ride along below the east cliffs," Slade replied. "Want to have a look at them; they're an interesting formation. Hope nobody takes a shot at me."

"Don't worry about that," said Jethro. "Everybody here knows you· now, and everybody thinks mighty well of you. The other day, you made a lot of friends, son.

"But," he added with a burst of shrewdness, "I've a notion you made some bad enemies, too. Look out for 'em."

"I will," Slade promised and meant it; very likely, he thought, Jethro Persinger had the right of it.

"Stop for more coffee on your way back," Jethro said. Young Nate smiled and seconded the invitation.

Slade rode slowly in the shadow of the cliffs, studying their peculiar striated surface and unusual coloring, the blotches and bands of vivid green, chocolate, brown and smoldering red standing out against the predominant pale gray background. He quickly noticed that for a distance of nearly a quarter of a mile from their bases westward the soil was productive of but very scanty vegetation, at striking variance with the luxuriant growth farther on.

"Yes, those rocks have undergone a great deal of weathering," he told Shadow. "For perhaps a million years or more they have eroded particles which fall and are carried by the wind, until the surface here is quite likely covered to a depth of a great many feet. That's why hardly anything grows on it—it's eroded stone."

The soil was spongy farther out from the cliffs and Shadow's hoofs sank deep. Near the cliff base, however, it was firmer, so Slade rode close to the towering wall, the crest of which often overhung. Finally he dismounted, dug into the earth with his hands and ran the grains through his fingers. They had a clay-like odor but were much more like sand than clay. Rocking back on his heels he rolled a cigarette and gazed across the valley, the concentration furrow deep between his black brows, a sure sign El Halcon was doing some hard thinking.

He was. For once again that illusive chord of memory

stirred, but refused to reveal anything tangible. Slade was becoming more and more convinced that in some manner those rainbowed cliffs held the answer to the mystery which plagued him; but they were evidently loath to divulge it.

The cliffs themselves were undoubtedly syenite feldspar, but as feldspars are estimated to make up fifty percent of the igneous rocks and sixteen percent of the sedimentary ones, that was a rather broad field from which to try to draw conclusions.

Mounting, he rode on for several miles. Always conditions were the same, the towering cliffs, the broad belt of unproductive land at their base. After a while he turned Shadow's head and rode back the way he had come, thoroughly perplexed and in anything but a good temper.

As he rode, he studied the crest of the cliffs, trying to estimate the rate of erosion throughout the ages, which could be significant.

It was the fact that he was giving attention to the cliff tops that saved him. Suddenly from overhead sounded a dull boom, a rending and rumbling. Slade saw a vast shadow rushing down toward him.

Instantly his voice rang out—"Trail, Shadow! Trail!"

The great black bounded forward on racing feet and immediately in his rear, a huge mass of rock struck the valley floor with a crash that quivered the mountains, spraying horse and rider with stinging fragments of stone.

It took Slade several hundred yards to get the frantic animal under control. Finally he pulled him to a halt, blowing and snorting, turned in the saddle and gazed back at the dust cloud rising from a wide area covered with broken stone. The palms of his hands were moist and a cold sweat beaded his temples.

"Shadow," he said in a strained voice, "if I hadn't been looking up right when I was, we'd be under that. Whe-e-ew! Dodging slugs is bad enough, but the side of a mountain! Gentlemen, hush!"

It didn't take Slade long to figure how the business was worked. When Sid Claxton repeated his words, "A look at the cliffs," in the bull-bellow he used for normal conversation, the wrong pair of ears heard, that was all. Then somebody circled through the hills and reached the cliff tops ahead of him. Somebody thoroughly familiar with conditions in the valley and who knew he would ride close to the cliffs where the ground was firmer. Then the hellion picked a strategic spot and planted a few sticks of dynamite that would bring down a section of overhang. From his point of vantage he was able to follow the progress of his intended victim down the valley, very likely by the sound of his horse's hoofs.

"Nice timing, too," he told Shadow. "The sidewinder knows how to handle explosives. Must have cut his fuse almighty short and had to hightail to get in the clear before the dynamite cut loose. Hope he fell down and didn't make it. Too much to hope for, though, I reckon. Let's go, horse, I've had enough of this infernal crack in the hills for a while."

The Persingers had heard the explosion, as doubtless had everybody else in the valley. Slade told them what happened.

"Told you to watch out for the skunks, that they'd be laying for you," old Jethro reminded.

"Yes, but I didn't pay enough heed to your warning," Slade replied. "I was careless, and came close to paying for my carelessness. After that drygulching from the cliff top I should have been on the lookout for some kind of skullduggery."

"Guess nobody can think of everything," nodded Jethro. "Here's your coffee, steaming hot, and Nate's got fried chicken ready in the skillet. Reckon you need a bite after all that excitement. Be careful riding back to town tonight; getting dark already."

He regarded Slade curiously for a moment. "I took that package to the Widow Price while you were gone, just a hop and a skip to her place. Son, did you know what was in that package?"

Slade smilingly shook his head.

"Two thousand dollars!" exclaimed Jethro. "Son, can't you tell us who sent all that money? It'll sure mean a lot to the poor woman and will tide her over the winter fine.

Can't you tell us who sent it?"

Still smiling, Slade shook his head. "I promised not to," he replied. "All I'm at liberty to tell you is that it was sent by a man who is going about doing good."

"Going about doing good," old Jethro repeated in a solemn voice. "That was said of our Blessed Lord in the days of old, 'He went about doing good!'"

ELEVEN

SLADE SPENT SOME TIME with the Persingers and it was late when he reached Vereda. He stabled his horse and repaired to the Diamond Flush. When he entered the saloon, he swept a swift glance over the room, hoping to catch an expression of surprise, perhaps consternation, on some face, and saw none. Rex Masters was not in evidence, but Blaine Webb was behind the bar at the other end, checking the till. Slade spotted an empty space near the end of the bar and, sauntered to it. Webb turned at that moment, a handful of silver slipped from his grasp and cascaded to the floor. With an oath he stopped to retrieve the coins and when he straightened up, his face was very red.

"Darn my clumsiness, anyhow," he growled in a thick voice. "How are you, Slade?"

"Things going wrong?" Slade asked sympathetically.

"One of those nights when everything goes wrong," Webb replied morosely. "Have a drink with me; maybe it'll change the luck."

A bartender filled two glasses. Slade nodded his thanks and sipped his. Webb raised his drink with a hand that trembled a little and downed it at a gulp.

"That should help," he said. "Blast it! there it goes again!" as the glass slid through his fingers and bounced off the bar.

"I'm about ready to give up," he said as he retrieved it and called for another drink.

The first one had apparently steadied his nerves, for he got the second down without incident. He grinned at Slade and went back to the till.

Slade lingered over his drink, smoked a cigarette and then, with a wave of his hand to Webb, departed. Ten minutes later found him in Doctor Austin's office. The old practitioner shook hands warmly and put coffee on to heat.

"Well, how goes it?" he asked, sitting down and producing his pipe.

"Not too good," Slade admitted.

"It's a mess," grunted Doc, stuffing his pipe. "We'll be lucky if we come out of it without really serious trouble. Just a match to the powder keg, and away we go."

"And somebody appears quite deft with matches," Slade observed. "Doc, I'd like to get the lowdown on folks hereabouts. Are there any newcomers in the section?"

"Well," said Austin, after his pipe was drawing to his satisfaction, "Well, let's see, now. There's young Bob Lambert who took over the Bradded L when his uncle died. He's sort of a newcomer—worked over around Laredo, I gather—but he used to visit here some when the old man was alive. Old Bass Hogadorn moved in a year or so back with his Rocking H outfit. He was formerly located up to the north, the other side of the county line, but lots of folks here knew him. You could hardly call him a newcomer in the real sense of the word, I reckon. Oh, yes, there's Blaine Webb and Rex Masters who showed up here about a year back, bought the Diamond Flush saloon, and the Diamond W spread, as they call it—changed the brand —from old Tom Haggerty after they got going good with the saloon. Guess that's about all—mostly oldtimers here, whose fathers and sometimes their grandfathers were here before them."

"Webb, Masters," Slade repeated. "Where are they from, do you know?"

"Understand they came down from the Panhandle," Doc replied. "Had a holding up there but got tired of fighting blizzards and tornadoes, like a lot of folks up there."

Slade nodded and rolled a cigarette, his eyes thoughtful.

"Yes, I guess that's about all, aside from the farmers," Doc repeated. "Ring any bells?"

"None definitely, that's certain," Slade replied. "What's got me thoroughly puzzled is what is behind this row; I have about arrived at the conclusion that somebody is deliberately endeavoring to heighten the friction between the two factions. Why? Suppose for the sake of the argument, it came to a showdown fight between the farmers and the ranchers; who would eventually lose?"

"The farmers," replied Austin. "They'd be hopelessly outnumbered and with conditions unfavorable to them."

"Yes. And those who remained alive after the row was over would pull out, leaving the valley untenanted, making it possible for somebody to acquire it and doubtless at a very low price."

"It's a valuable bit of property, now that it's irrigated," Doc commented.

"Yes, but not of such value as by any stretch of the imagination to justify the risks involved in its acquisition by such methods as are being employed. Somebody is walking in the shadow of the noose. Somebody, I'd say, who is playing for big stakes."

"And what are the stakes?"

"That's what I'd like to know," Slade replied morosely. "I seem to be beating my brains out against a stone wall. And what makes it the more aggravating is the fact that in the back of my mind something keeps hinting that I should know what the stakes are; then it slips away like water held in the clenched hand. At times I have a feeling that I'm going loco."

"Could be," Doc agreed cheerfully. "In fact, I think you're already a bit touched in the head and have been for quite a while. A highly competent engineer fooling around with a Ranger job!"

"Perhaps," Slade smiled, "but I get a lot of satisfaction every now and then from Ranger work. Besides, it's an exciting game, pitting your wits against those who employ off-color practices."

"With death as the forfeit," Doc observed grimly. "Oh, well, I reckon you'll come out on top; you always do."

Which was encouraging, but of which Slade himself at the moment was not sure. He had plenty of faith in himself but the present situation appeared to be very much of a stalemate, with quite probably the other player holding the trump cards, his real ace in the hole the fact that he, Slade, had no definite notion as to who his opponent might be. Oh, well, luck was supposed to favor the virtuous; maybe it would.

Since the attempt to murder Sid Claxton, Slade always approached his room over the Diamond Flush warily, although he hardly expected a repeat performance. Nothing happened when he cautiously opened the door and he slept well despite the not inconsiderable racket below.

When he entered the saloon for breakfast the following morning, he was surprised to find Sid Claxton seated at a table and putting away a hefty surrounding.

"Had to come in to arrange for a train of cars," Claxton announced. "Figure to ship a small herd next week; need a mite of ready cash. Take a load off your feet. I'll be ready to ride back to the spread in the early afternoon; suppose you ride with me. Right! I'll meet you here."

Slade wandered around the town for a while and neither heard nor saw anything of particular interest. He was ready and waiting when Claxton entered the saloon, called for a drink and announced his intention of leaving at once. While he was discussing his plans, Rex Masters appeared in riding costume.

"Figure to be at your place for the meeting tonight," he told Claxton. "I'll ride with you."

Slade got the rig on Shadow and they rode out of town together, conversing on various rangeland matters. When they came opposite the Diamond W ranchhouse, Masters said,

"I want to pick up some papers. Come on in for coffee and some cake; we've got a good cook."

"You're darn right, you have," old Sid agreed with enthusiasm. "I've sampled his helpin's."

Several cowhands were idling about the grounds. Slade noted the unsavory Pete Houck who evidently didn't want

any part of Sid Claxton, for he sidled away and disappeared
behind the bunkhouse.

The living room of the ranchhouse was small but tastefully furnished. One wall was devoted to bookshelves filled
with fat volumes; evidently Webb and Masters did a good
deal of reading.

Just as evidently their taste did not run to light fiction;
nearly all of the books dealt with serious subjects. Slade
noted some of the titles with interest. There was Leith's
"World Minerals" and "Economic Aspects of Geology,"
Spurr's "Political and Commercial Geology," The Bureau
of Standards' circular, "Light Metals and Alloys," Young's
"Elements of Mining," Peele's "Mining Engineer's Hand-
book," Arkose's "Petrology," and more of a similar nature.
An unusual collection for cattlemen, Slade thought.

His gaze rested on another fat tome, "Bauxite and its
Derivatives."

Suddenly the little devils of laughter that always seemed
to dance in the depths of his cold eyes were still and very
serious devils.

TWELVE

THE RANCH OWNERS WERE ALREADY begin-
ning to gather when they reached the Cross C ranchhouse.
Slade was introduced to several he had not as yet met and
felt that he was getting a very thorough once-over. Verna
greeted him with enthusiasm.

"I hope you plan to spend the night," she remarked
insinuatingly as they stood alone on the veranda.

"Are the balcony and the windows still there?" he
asked.

"They're still there," she replied, her eyes dancing.

"Okay, then," he said, laughter in his own eyes.

Old Sid insisted that everybody eat before getting down
to business, and the big dining room was crowded with
owners, their range bosses and older hands.

Blaine Webb was the last to arrive, having checked up before leaving the Diamond Flush in the care of his head bartender. With him was the Diamond W range boss and, somewhat to Slade's surprise, Pete Houck.

As the meeting got under way, there was quickly evidence of a strong difference of opinion. Some of the ranchers insisted vigorously that the farmers were responsible for the recent outrages. Others thought otherwise, bolstering their contention by pointing out the murder of Abner Price and Sid Claxton's belief that it was not a farmer or one of their emissaries who attempted his life in his room over the Diamond Flush. Still others admitted they didn't know what to think.

Claxton nodded to Slade, who outlined his reasons for believing the farmers guiltless of wrong. The ranchers listened intently, nodded from time to time. When he had finished, Pete Houck stood up.

"Slade makes out a purty good case for the nesters," he said in his whining nasal voice. "But remember, he's got a sort of off-colored reputation himself. So—"

"Sit down and shut up!" roared old Sid. "If you wasn't a guest in my house I'd beat your blasted brains out. Webb, Masters, why don't you teach that mangy horned toad to tighten the latigo on his jaw?"

Houck subsided. Masters and Webb shook their heads at him disapprovingly. Slade smiled thinly and said nothing.

After more discussion, the ranchers agreed not to make any move against the farmers until some overt act was definitely proved against them.

The meeting broke up. Many of the ranchers paused to shake hands with Slade. Crusty old Bass Hogadorn looked him up and down with his rheumy eyes.

"Figure you got a head on your shoulders, young feller," he said. "You can count on me stringing along with you. I believe you have the right notion. Hope you'll see fit to stay with us; we can use men like you. Sign up with Sid and settle down here." With a nod, he strode to the door, upright and vigorous despite his seventy-odd years, favoring Pete Houck with a contemptuous glance as he passed out. A glance, Slade noted, that took in Houck's employers as well. Squire Hogadorn evidently subscribed to the saying that birds of a feather flock together.

"Bass has sense," Claxton remarked, after his guests had departed. "He's all right, and he can hold more hard likker and cuss better'n any man in the county."

Verna turned to Slade. "And now, Walt, sing and play for us," she urged. "Your music is—inspiring."

"Okay, if you feel in the need of inspiration," Slade smiled.

As he sang, old Sid's eyes grew dreamy, Verna's very bright. "Inspired?" he asked as he paused for breath.

"Yes, very much so," she replied. "Devastatingly so!"

"And now for some more coffee," said Claxton. "Believe I can stand a snack, too. All that palavering made me hungry."

Slade sat smoking in silence while Verna prepared the coffee. All in all, he was fairly pleased with the outcome of the meeting. He hadn't told the ranchers much they didn't already know, but he had put over his point by the power of his personality. People listen to an honest and forceful man, even though perhaps inclined to disagree with him, at first. Anyhow, he had won something like a truce, for the time being.

Not that he had definitely won the fight. Far from it. The ranchers were inclined to go along with him, but it would take little to put them on the prod again, and Slade felt that somebody would work very hard to produce something that would get their bristles up. Well, perhaps he would be able to anticipate and forestall it. At least he was getting a very definite idea as to what was the motive back of the seemingly unexplainable actions.

Strange how things worked out. How a seemingly unimportant meeting and move could provide the lead he so sorely needed. The tool carves the statue and the hand holds the tool, but the spirit guides the hand. That Slade firmly believed, unexplainable though it seemed. Not being overly burdened with ego, he did not stop to reflect that his own keen perceptions and his ability to analyze and correlate apparently inconsequential acts, happenings and facts were largely responsible for his success in following what he was wont to call hunches. His hunches were really the result of accurate deduction translated into action.

THIRTEEN

SLADE AND CLAXTON RODE the Cross C range the following morning. Slade was even more impressed by its excellence as old Sid pointed out salient features.

There were plenty of fine cattle grazing on the good grass and Slade quickly concluded that the acreage was stocked to capacity. Far to the north they reached a terrain where the grass was even better than average, but a very large stretch lay untenanted by cows.

"No water," Claxton replied to his question. "Grass is fine but not a waterhole, creek or spring for miles and the cows won't stray onto it."

Slade nodded thoughtfully, studying the land with its lush growth. He turned and gazed at the hills to the west, estimating the distance covered in the course of the ride, triangulating their position, and arrived at the conclusion that a few miles farther on would bring them opposite the big lake in the volcanic cup, the lake which supplied the farmers with their irrigation water that, compared to the volume of water in the old crater, was very small. The lake was undoubtedly fed by great springs deep in the earth. Springs that would never run dry and which provided a constant overflow which emptied itself by way of some subterranean channel.

"Guess we might as well turn back," Claxton said. "Nothing more to see up this way."

"Mind if we ride a couple of miles or so farther?" Slade asked.

"Okay with me, if you want to," Claxton replied, casting a curious glance at his companion.

They rode on at a steady pace, Slade constantly studying the hills to the west. Finally he drew rein.

"This will be far enough," he announced. His gaze swept over the grasslands, nothing that here the grass was even more lush than farther south, turned to once more study the hills, the slopes of which were grown with heavy brush that looked like a blue shadow in the distance. He turned in his saddle to face the rancher.

"Mr. Claxton," he said, "did you ever hear of something called an artesian well?"

"Why, yes, although I don't think I ever saw one," Claxton replied. "Shoot water up into the air, don't they? None in this section that I ever heard tell of."

"Well, there should be," Slade said. Claxton looked puzzled.

"Where?"

"Right here," Slade answered. "There should be a string of them right across the range to the east."

"Son, what the devil are you getting at?" demanded the puzzled cowman.

"Just this," Slade said. "Here you have thousands of unproductive acres, so far as cows are concerned. Land that is just going to waste. That condition could easily be remedied."

"How?" asked Claxton.

"By sinking a few artesian wells," Slade told him. "I'm willing to wager that beneath the land is a great subterranean reservoir under pressure. Tap it and you'll get all the water needed to make this acreage ideal for cattle raising. It'll cost you quite a bit, but will pay off big."

Old Sid looked deeply interested. "But how about rigs to drill them?" he asked. "Reckon the dinky little things folks use to drill kitchen wells wouldn't do."

"Hardly," Slade agreed, "but I can obtain rigs from Laredo pretty quickly, if you wish to go in for it."

"You feel sure there's water under the land?" Claxton asked.

"Yes, I'm sure," Slade replied. "In fact, I'm pretty sure there is a vast underground system all through west Texas, as folks will find out and take advantage of some day."

Subsequent events were to prove Walt Slade eminently correct in his surmise.

"Guess we might as well turn back," he suggested. "I've learned what I wanted to learn about this terrain."

Claxton nodded without speaking. In fact, he didn't speak until they had covered several miles of the homeward ride. Abruptly he turned in his saddle.

"Son, I've been thinking it over and I believe I'll string along with the notion," he said. "But what would happen if that lake up in the hills should go dry?"

"Nothing, so far as this terrain is concerned," Slade replied. "The springs, the source of the water, would continue to flow and keep the underground water under pressure. Hardly conceivable that they would go dry, for they are fed by underground rivers. Not likely that the lake would either, for that matter. That is unless," he added thoughtfully, "the retaining wall should happen to burst. Which any sort of even mild subterranean disturbance might cause it to do; it is far from thick, considering the volume of water it holds back."

"What would happen if it did?" Claxton asked.

"Well, for one thing it would sweep Vereda Valley clean from end to end," Slade replied seriously. "Might even give the town of Vereda a wetting, although I think that unlikely. Would be apt to dissipate over the prairie before it reached the town."

"Hmmm! I wouldn't want to be living in that consarned valley if there's a chance of that happening," observed Claxton. "But I tell you what, tomorrow, if it's okay with you, we'll ride to town and see if you can arrange for those drilling rigs."

"Okay with me," Slade replied.

"Then that's settled," said Claxton. "Let's go! I'm hungry!"

Both were hungry when they reached the ranchhouse about dusk and did ample justice to the repast set before them. Old Sid was full of the proposed project and discussed it at the table, with Verna an interested listener. He was tired after the long ride and soon stumped up the stairs to bed, leaving Slade and Verna alone in the living room.

"I don't know how you do it," the girl marvelled. "He

does everything you tell him to and relies on your judgment implicitly."

"Sort of runs in the family, doesn't it?" Slade smiled. Verna blushed a little and her eyes were shy.

"That's different," she said. "But Dad is usually very chary of taking advice from anybody and is usually contrary as a blue-nosed mule, as the boys say. I believe if you told him to jump off the roof, assuring him it would do him no harm, he'd do it."

"I won't put him to the test," Slade laughed. "Any advice I give him is for his own good."

"I'm sure of that. And me?"

"What do you think?"

She flashed him a sideways glance through her lashes. "I have no complaint, none at all, but I'm riding to town with you tomorrow. Remember, you promised to take me riding, and so far you haven't."

"We'll make it tomorrow," he said.

They did ride to town the following morning. Verna sat in the hotel lobby while they transacted their business at the telegraph office. Several messages clicked back and forth over the wires. Finally Slade passed Claxton a column of totalled figures.

"That's what it will cost," he said. "Can you swing it?"

Old Sid glanced at the total. "Sure," he said, "I've got a nest egg laid away. But I insist on one thing, that you take charge of the business and see it's handled right. That'll sign you up with me," he added with a chuckle. "And I sure hope you'll stay signed up. I'm going to have a snack and a drink and then head back to the ranch. Verna wants to stay in town for a while, if you'll ride back with her tonight."

"Be glad to," Slade answered. He sent a last message, got the answer.

"The rigs will be on your holding the first of next week," he announced.

"Okay," said Claxton. "See you tonight."

Slade returned to the hotel to join Verna. "Well, where do you want to ride?" he asked.

"You lead and I'll follow," she replied.

"Okay," Slade said. "How about riding up Vereda Valley?"

Verna's eyes widened a little. "You sure somebody won't shoot us?"

"I don't think so, especially with you along," Slade chuckled. "I want you to meet some friends of mine up there."

"You seem to have friends everywhere," she commented.

"That's covering a lot of territory," Slade said. "I fear you tend to exaggerate."

"Everywhere you go, then," she corrected, dimpling up at him. Slade laughed and they rode on. Now and then a farmer would pass on the way to town, recognize Slade and wave a cordial greeting, glancing curiously at Verna but making no remark.

They rode steadily until they reached the Persinger farmhouse. Father and son were at home. They greeted Slade warmly and were slightly flabbergasted when Slade performed the introductions. They quickly recovered their aplomb, however. Young Nate at once insisted on preparing something to eat.

"I'll help you," Verna said. "Oh, don't worry, I'm used to kitchens; cooking is woman's work."

Nate looked shy and embarrassed but offered no further protest. Slade and Jethro walked out to look over the crops.

"Well, how did you like them?" Slade asked Verna when, some time later, they rode back down the valley.

"They're fine people," she instantly replied. "Nate is shy, diffident, but he's sweet. He was telling me how he hoped to be an engineer some day."

"He will be," Slade stated positively. "You can rely on that."

Verna looked pensive. "I wonder," she said slowly, "I wonder if I could persuade Dad to lend him the money for his course."

"Wouldn't be surprised if you could," Slade answered, "but I'm going to tell you something that must be a secret between you and me."

"Another secret just between you and me?" Verna interrupted. "What is it this time?"

"Just this," Slade answered. "As I said, I don't think you'd have much trouble persuading your dad to advance the money, but—I don't think it will be necessary; Nate, I'm pretty sure, will be able to make the grade by himself. I won't tell you how just yet, for I am not positive that I'm right, but I'm sure enough to bet heavily on it. Anyhow, one way or another, Nate will get his chance. That I assure you, definitely."

Verna glanced up at the sternly handsome face, and her eyes were soft, glowing.

"Walt," she said, "do you always go about doing good for people?"

"I'm afraid not always, and not for everybody," he smiled, "but I try."

"And succeed," she said, with finality, "even where women are concerned. You're good for a woman, even though she knows she can't hope to hold you."

Slade laughed aloud. "Lucky for the woman," he said. "I fear an extended period would drive any woman loco."

"Doesn't have to be an extended period," Verna giggled, her eyes dancing. "Come on, I'll race you to the crest of that long rise."

"Go ahead," Slade agreed; "I'll give you a slight handicap."

Verna spoke to the big roan she was riding and he shot ahead at a fast gait. Shadow continued to pace sedately, although his ears slanted back a little and he gave a slight snort of protest. Slade watched the flying roan's progress, estimated the distance to the rise crest. The roan was already a good hundred yards to the front. Verna turned in her saddle.

"You'll never catch up!" she called gleefully.

"Think not?" Slade called back. His voice rang out, urgent, compelling.

"Trail, Shadow, trail!"

Instantly the great black extended himself. His steely legs shot back like steam pistons, he snorted, slugged his head above the bit, and fairly poured his long body over the ground. Who the devil did that scrawny critter ahead think he was? What did he think he was?

With astonishing rapidity, Shadow closed the distance. The rise crest was still a full two hundred yards distant when he flashed past the laboring roan with a snort of triumph. On the rise crest Slade pulled him to a halt and had a cigarette half rolled before the foaming roan came to a halt beside them, his sides heaving, breathing heavily.

"What a horse!" Verna marvelled. "I don't think he has an equal in all Texas. Nor anywhere else for that matter. He's wonderful!"

"He'll do," Slade said briefly, gazing at her with admiration. Her unruly red hair framed her little heart-shaped face in smoldering flame, her eyes sparkled and there was vivid color in her creamily tanned cheeks. Slade breathed deeply. She was something, too!

It was late when they reached the ranchhouse, after a dreamy ride under the stars. They found old Sid at a table covered with scribbled sheets.

"Son," he said, "I've been doing a bit of calc'lating. If things work out the way you say they will, I figure that what I'll gain from one season will more than pay the whole cost. After that, pure gravy."

He looked reflective, drummed on the table with the tip of his pencil.

"I was wondering," he said, "if it wouldn't pay the boys to the east and farther north to do some drilling, too."

"In my opinion it would," Slade replied. "As I said before, I'm convinced that there is a great underground water system covering all this section. However, they'd have to drill much deeper. The main body of the reservoir is undoubtedly under your north pastures, which accounts for the lushness of the grass. The water, under pressure, works upward through the earth and holds rainwater in suspension. That condition would not prevail elsewhere."

Old Sid gazed at him curiously. "You sure express yourself out of the ordinary and know a lot about such things for a—cowhand," he remarked.

"Perhaps I'm observant," Slade smiled.

"Evidently," Claxton conceded dryly. Across the room, his pretty daughter laughed.

"You're on the payroll, son, from the first of the week,

but I don't expect you to do anything till the rigs get here. Take it easy for a few days."

"Thank you, sir, I do feel like fooling around town a little," Slade replied.

"Lots of pretty *senoritas* in the cantinas," Verna observed airily.

"Outside them, too," Slade returned, with meaning. Verna slanted him a glance through her lashes and smiled.

FOURTEEN

SLADE RODE TO TOWN the following afternoon. At a general store he purchased a heavy trowel, a small wooden box with a sliding lid, some wrapping paper and some twine. All of which he stowed in his saddle pouches. In the dark hours before the dawn the next morning he slipped quietly from his room. Reaching the street he paused, glancing up and down. Making sure nobody was watching his movements, he hurried to the stable where Shadow resided, got the rig on the big black and rode north into Vereda Valley. On the crest of a rise he pulled up and sat for some time, his eyes fixed on the stretch of trail he had traversed. It stretched silent and deserted, shimmered by the starlight.

Satisfied that he was not wearing a tail, he rode on. Full daylight found him skirting the base of the eastern cliffs. He rode some miles up the valley, studying the soil and the cliffs, glancing back the way he had come.

Well up the valley he dismounted and, using the trowel, dug deep into the spongy soil. He ran the hard grains through his fingers, studied them, dug deeper. Always the soil was the same.

"And I'll bet a hatful of *pesos* the bed is thirty or forty feet thick," he told Shadow. "I'm practically certain I'm right, but we'll make sure and confirm it officially."

Working in the depths of the hole, he filled the wooden box. He took a sheet of paper from his saddle pouch and covered it with writing in a firm, clear hand. He folded the paper, slipped it into the box and closed the sliding lid. With the wrapping paper and twine he securely wrapped and tied the box, addressing it to a friend in the mineral division of the great university at the state capital. Then, well satisfied with his morning's work, he rode back to town and entered the post office.

"Send it first class," he told the postmaster; "there's a letter inside."

"Feels like there's rocks in it, too," grunted the postmaster, hefting it and slipping it onto his scales. He tore off a number of stamps from a sheet.

"Expensive way to send a package," he remarked, affixing the stamps. Slade smiled and did not comment.

The chore attended to, he headed for the Diamond Flush and something to eat, which he was sorely in need of. Blaine Webb and Rex Masters were both present. They nodded and went on talking together in low tones. After a while the latter strolled over to Slade's table and dropped into a chair.

"See you are still with us, Mr. Slade," he said cheerfully.

"Yes," Slade agreed, the thing being fairly obvious.

"Going to coil your twine here?" Masters asked casually.

"I've signed up with Mr. Claxton," Slade replied, refraining from mentioning in what capacity.

"A good man to work for," nodded Masters. "A bit hottempered and quick, but okay. You did well to get in with him." He chuckled.

"Your first meeting, I understand, wasn't exactly a friendly one," he commented.

"Just a slight disagreement that meant nothing," Slade answered. "We got along all right after a bit."

"Evidently," Masters conceded. "He appears to think a great deal of you."

"I hope so," Slade replied, and meant it. Masters nodded.

"Enjoy your dinner," he said. "I'll send over a drink." With a nod and a smile he sauntered back to his partner.

Slade fooled around the town the rest of the day, and learned nothing he considered significant. An uneasy truce existed for the moment, but he labored under no illusion that it would be permanent unless some drastic happening brought the two factions together.

"And it looks like the only drastic happening possible is a troop of Rangers being sent in to keep the peace, which the sheriff certainly can't do," he told Shadow gloomily. "Which would mean I fell down on a job. And which," he added grimly, "I have no intention of doing. Maybe I'll get a break."

The drill rig and the men to operate it arrived on schedule Monday morning and was at once loaded on big freight wagons and trundled to the scene of operations, the Cross C north pasture. Slade decided to drill five wells and designated the spots. The rig was set up, the steam boiler stoked and the heavy steel bit began churning into the earth.

Day after day the drilling continued. The Cross C hands were busy digging waterholes to hold the expected flow. Slade studied the prevailing slope of the land.

"The overflow will scour out a stream which will flow north and benefit the spreads there," he told Claxton.

But as the drilling continued and the bit bored deeper and deeper, old Sid, experienced only in shallow kitchen wells, grew anxious.

"You're sure you're not making a mistake, son?" he asked dubiously.

"This young feller ain't making any mistake," said the rig foreman, who overheard. "We'll hit it in another day or two. Don't you figure so, Slade?"

"You are about right, I'd say," the Ranger answered.

Slade's estimate was correct. The following afternoon they struck water and a stream spouted more than twenty feet into the air and continued to spout. The rig was moved to another spot and the drilling resumed.

Slade was also right in his prediction that the overflow would begin scouring out a bed and flowing northward.

"The boys up there are getting a break," chuckled Claxton, rubbing his hands together complacently. "She's making a creek, all right, digging in deeper all the time."

"In a million years or so it may form another Grand Canyon," Slade remarked smilingly. Claxton shook his head.

"Too long to stick around," he said. "Maybe I'll come back to see it, though."

"The theory of reincarnation is the first article of faith among nearly one quarter of the human race, and this not the most foolish quarter," Slade replied. "Maybe you'll make it."

Slade studied the embryo creek that would be greatly augmented by the succeeding wells. Should be quite a sizeable stream once all five were pouring their overflow into it. He raised his eyes to the terrain to the north. As far as his gaze would carry, the gentle slope to the north continued, but the ground was practically level east and west. The creek, once bedded, would follow an almost direct course for so long as the trend of the watershed remained the same. He regarded the far distances and arrived at a conclusion.

He knew there were a number of spreads between where Claxton's holding ended and the barrier hills many miles to the north. Some to the west, others to the east. Eventually the new stream would extend to the northern hills, scouring out its channel where the least physical resistance would offer, which to all appearances would be not far from the western hills. And as he speculated the twinkling film spreading over the grassland, he evolved a plan. A plan he believed might well prove a valuable asset in time of need.

As they rode back to the ranchhouse, Slade questioned Claxton relative to the location and conditions of the spreads to the north, and what he learned strengthened his resolve to put the plan into effect.

The following morning, early, he got the rig on Shadow and rode north. At the site of the drilling he paused to chat with the rig foreman.

"Coming along fine," said that worthy. "This job is play to some I've tackled in my time. No thick rock to pound through, no drilling guesswork test holes because you don't know for sure where your underground source is located. All you got to do here is just keep going straight down. Yep, you sure figured right when you said the reservoir would extend under this whole stretch. And I figure, too, that you're right when you say there's a great underground water system covering this whole southwest Texas section. You ain't got any business following a cow's tail for a living; you ought to be an engineer."

"Maybe I will be," Slade smiled.

"I doubt it," the driller disagreed cheerfully. "Once a cowman, always a cowman. Be seeing you."

Chuckling to himself, Slade rode on north. With a slight variation, the driller might be nearer right than he knew.

As he rode, Slade studied the land, and time and again his glance strayed to the grim hills flanking the range on the west. Even in the bright sunshine they seemed to frown, gathering unto themselves the shadows and sheltering them in their silent gorges and their tangled thickets. And they seemed to glower at the quiet rangeland at their feet. Sunshine and peace were not for them. They were and always had been sanctuary for hunted men, the abiding place of the lawless. Prowling Indian, marauders from Mejico, smuggler, rustler and killer had trod their furtive trails, always a threat and a menace to the law-abiding. And now their dark depths hid whåt well might be the greatest threat of all.

"But you can be whipped, darn you!" he apostrophized the somber cliffs. "Before I'm finished with you, you'll make this section a really decent place for decent folks to live. You'll see!" He rode on, and ignored the hills.

After he had covered quite a few miles, he turned Shadow's nose to the east.

"Over there and not too far, according to what Claxton told me, is Jonathan Butler's ranchhouse," he explained to Shadow. "He's the first gent we want to have a little gab with."

Butler had been present at the meeting in Claxton's ranchhouse and remembered Slade.

"Glad to see you, son," he greeted the Ranger. "Light

off and cool your saddle; you're just in time for a surroundin'. Cook's already bellered."

After they finished eating, Slade broached the subject
which had occasioned his visit. He reviewed the results
of the drilling on Claxton's range.

"And that excess water will keep on flowing north for-
ever," he concluded. "But water always follows the path
of least resistance. And by so doing, it will bypass some
of the spreads up this way, including yours. However, with
a little work you can cause it to flow in more of a zig-zag
course and benefit everybody. A little ditching and em-
banking is all that is necessary. Get the notion, Mr.
Butler?"

"Reckon I do," the rancher replied. "Son, you got a
head on your shoulders. We'll do just as you say. Tell
you what, suppose we ride up to Lex Duncan's place and
give him the lowdown? We'll have Lex pass the word
along to the other boys. You can ride back with me and
spend the night here. Okay?"

Slade agreed and they set out. Duncan also proved
receptive to the idea and promised to pass the word along.
As a result, Slade rode back to the Cross C ranchhouse
the following morning very well satisfied with the way his
plan had worked out.

His purpose had not been altogether altruistic. He
wanted the ranchers to benefit to the greatest extent from
the unexpected windfall—or waterfall—but he also knew
that his action would strengthen his influence over the
cattlemen, which could prove highly important if the
possible, even probable showdown between the two factions should develop.

"Every little bit helps," he told Shadow as they jogged
home. "Get folks feeling they're sort of under obligation
to you and you're in a much better position to ask a favor
when you need one. Horse, I've a notion things are going
to work out after all—maybe!"

Finally the drilling was finished and the drillers departed grateful for the handsome bonus handed them by
the highly pleased rancher.

"Would appear my chore is also finished," Slade said.

"Not by a jugful!" declared Claxton. "You've got to stick around and see to it that everything works out okay; something might happen. Oh, you're not going to get away from me for a while!"

There had been considerable skepticism among the cattlemen when the drilling started. Some had openly scoffed at the project. Now, however, men vied with one another to congratulate Claxton and praise Slade for his acumen.

Among the foremost was Rex Masters, the ranch and saloon owner.

"A fine chore, Mr. Slade, a very fine chore," he said, looking the Ranger up and down with a critical eye. "How in the world did you hit on it?"

"I once saw a somewhat similar formation over in Arizona," Slade replied. Which was perfectly true. "From the look of the land I thought there should be water under it. You know the excess water from that lake up in the hills has to drain off somewhere. I scouted around in the valley to see if there were signs of the underground channel running in that direction and didn't find any. Had a narrow escape up there, though. A whole section of cliff sluffed off right over where I was riding. It was a close call."

"I imagine it was," nodded Masters. "Must have startled you somewhat."

"Well, it wasn't exactly easy on the nerves," Slade conceded, and with truth.

"Freezes and thaws loosen the rocks and sometimes cause them to fall," Masters observed. Slade nodded agreement.

Privately he wondered just how much Masters believed. If he had swallowed what he was told, it might serve to somewhat allay his suspicions of El Halcon and his reputation for horning in on good things other folks had started.

However, Slade was not at all sure that Masters had swallowed it. He had an uneasy suspicion that Rex Masters was a hard man to fool. Back of those pale eyes and the handsome, impassive face was a hair-trigger brain that analyzed and evaluated and arrived at correct decisions.

But, as it always seemed the owlhoot brand did, he made a slip. Slade had become interested in Blaine Webb the night he turned from the till and dropped the handful of coins in his obvious shock and confusion at coming face to face with the man he had reason to believe was dead, crushed under the rock fall in Vereda Valley. Then Rex Masters made the fatal mistake of inviting him into the Diamond W ranchhouse where Slade saw shelves loaded with books only of interest to a mining engineer or operator. Also, the title of one of the volumes had stirred to life, with understanding, that illusive chord of memory which had plagued the Ranger.

The books were evidence that either Webb or Masters, in his opinion the latter, possibly both, were the only individuals he had met in the section who would be able to read aright the significance of the weathered cliffs that walled the valley on the east, and the extensive erosive deposits at their base. A fortune just waiting to be claimed! At present the property of the valley farmers. No wonder the two hellions were willing to commit murder to acquire it.

Through the smoke of his cigarette he studied the two men who stood conversing in low tones at the bar. Blaine Webb was a hard man, looked it and acted it. Rex Masters, Slade believed, was an even harder, and neither looked nor acted like one. A somewhat far-fetched comparison would be the big, blustering rattlesnake, obtrusive, and deadly, and the innocuous looking and unobstrusive little coral snake, even more deadly, that struck without warning.

He wondered what was the man's background. Not that it made any difference at the moment; Slade's interest was in his acts in the section, not elsewhere, yet.

Probably a brilliant engineer or technician who somehow had forsaken the straight trail despite his advantages of intelligence and education; he had met the sort before. Well, no telling where the lightning would strike. If the criminal element ran to a distinctive pattern, the work of a peace officer would be much simpler. It didn't.

Leaving the saloon, Slade headed for the post office, where he found a letter from the capital awaiting him. As he read the contents, his eyes glowed. He carefully stowed the letter away and walked to the livery stable to commune with Shadow, who was always an interested listener and did not interrupt save for an occasional snort.

"Hit the nail squarely on the head," he told the big black. "My diagnosis, which was to a certain extent guesswork, proved correct. Looks like Nate Persinger will get his wish, all right, barring unforeseen complications."

Unforeseen complications were to make themselves manifest in short order.

FIFTEEN

Two days later Slade and Verna rode to town. They met Jethro Persinger on the street; his face was grave.

"The boys are all het up," he announced. "They've been told that those wells you drilled on Mr. Claxton's land will drain off the water from the lake and leave us high and dry."

"That's utter nonsense!" Slade snapped. "Those wells won't lower the level of the underground reservoir by as much as an inch, much less the lake, which will not be affected at all. If they even tapped the lake water, which they don't, they would still not affect it any more than does your irrigation flume. Even if the springs which feed the lake ceased to flow, which they won't, it would take years for the wells to drain the lake, did they tap it."

"That's what Nate says," nodded Jethro, "and I figure he knows what he's talking about. But I think you'd better ride up the valley and have a talk with the boys."

"And I'll ride with you," Verna instantly volunteered. "Nate has sense."

"That'll be fine," said Jethro.

"Just who started that rumor, do you know?" Slade asked as they got under way.

"I don't know," Jethro replied. "One of our younger fellers was in the Diamond Flush—us older fellers never go there—and he heard folks there talking about it."

"I see," Slade said. "Guess he was meant to hear."

"Walt, what does it mean?" Verna asked.

"A deliberate attempt to foment trouble," Slade answered. "We'll talk about it later."

In the course of the afternoon they visited many homes and Slade carefully explained how ridiculous the rumor was. When they headed for home, after coffee and a snack with the Persingers, which again Nate and Verna prepared together, he felt that he had allayed the farmers' fears.

"Walt," Verna said as they neared the Cross C ranchhouse, "why is somebody trying to stir up trouble between the farmers and the cowmen?"

"Because they want Vereda Valley," he replied.

"Because the land is valuable now that it's irrigated?"

He hesitated. "Okay," he finally said, "I feel like confiding in somebody and I know I can trust you not to talk."

"You certainly should know it by now," she retorted.

"Guess I should," he agreed. "No, it is not the irrigated land they want, but the cliffs which wall the valley on the east and are part of the farmers' holdings."

"The cliffs?"

"Yes, and the land at their base; it's worth a fortune. Here."

He handed her the letter from the capital and struck a match so she could read the few words it contained.

She looked up, a little pucker between her brows. "And it's really valuable?"

"Yes, and those beds are of vast extent and, I believe, even thicker than the world-famous ones in Arkansas. You see now what I meant when I said Nate Persinger wouldn't need to borrow money to acquire the education he desires."

"I'm so glad, for him," she said. "But who is trying to stir up the trouble?"

"I can't name names just yet, because I have no proof that will stand up in court, but I hope to get it, sooner or later."

"You will," she predicted confidently. She shuddered a little. "And meanwhile, you are in grave danger, are you not?"

He shrugged his broad shoulders. "The danger can bide, to employ a word that is fast becoming archaic," he replied.

"I think," she said slowly, "that I'm beginning to understand what you meant when you said you'd drive any woman loco. And not pleasantly."

Slade laughed. But he felt that if things kept on like they were, he would be the one to go loco.

What next, he wondered as he sat that night, smoking and thinking. Old Sid had gone to bed, and so had Verna, tired out by the long ride, and he was alone in the quiet living room. He felt he could sympathize with a bee keeper trying to maintain peace between two angry swarms, running from hive to hive to thrust back potential trouble makers, and sometimes getting stung himself. With some unseen hellion continually poking the rear of the hive with a stick.

His sense of humor came to the rescue and he chuckled. Very quickly, however, he was grave again as he pondered the problem that confronted him. He believed he had frustrated the latest attempt to stir up trouble, with Verna's help. Her shrewd little brain knew exactly what to do. While he talked with the farmers, she worked on the women, with results. Slade's keen ears caught a fragment of conversation between two wives—

"Yes, I've seen her before, riding in town, and I thought she was a mighty pretty girl and looked like a nice one; but I never dreamed she could be so common. I believe every word she says."

Slade understood the meaning of the word "common" as used by these Kentuckians and knew it to be very complimentary.

What next? It was logical to think that an attempt would be made to get the ranchers on the prod, but how? He believed that he had convinced them that the farmers were not widelooping their cattle nor poisoning their waterholes. Just as he had quieted their fear of the irrigation water running across the land. He knew he had convinced Sid Claxton, and Claxton's influence with the cattlemen was not small. Claxton was using that water now and glad to get it.

Gradually he arrived at a conclusion. Yes, that would very likely be it, and the farmers would be blamed. Their recent disquietude over the supposed danger to the lake from the artesian wells would lend credence to the assumption. A little clever propaganda, subtly insinuated, by the two horned toads would fan the fires.

It was one of the oldest outlaw tricks, setting two factions against each other, with each blaming the other for whatever happened. Sometimes erupting into such devastation as the Higgins-Horrel feud or the Lincoln County war.

Yes, an old trick, simple but effective. Slade had encountered the like before. But never, he believed, had he been up against such smooth operators as Rex Masters and Blaine Webb. Both enjoyed an excellent reputation. Both had friends among the cattlemen, and they managed to stay on good terms with the farmers. Nobody suspected them. Nobody had any reason to. If he tried to bring a charge against them he would be laughed out of court.

Gazing through the mist of his cigarette smoke he evolved an expedient that might possibly tend to substantiate his conclusion as to how the next try would be made. The following morning, while talking with Claxton, he deftly steered the conversation to a matter they had already tentatively discussed, letting old Sid make the decision.

"Yes," he agreed, "I think it would be a good notion to dig out a few more waterholes down this way and fill them from the irrigation creek."

"I'll set the boys to work on 'em right away," said Claxton.

"A little dynamite with which to blow the holes would expedite the chore and make it easier for them," Slade suggested casually. "I suppose they know how to handle the stuff?"

"Yes, Clem Yates, the range boss, knows all about it. He'll handle it right," Claxton assured him.

"Then suppose I drive the light wagon to town and get some," Slade volunteered.

"That'll be fine," replied Claxton. "Tell old Thompson to put it on my account. How much do you figure we'll need?"

"I'd say one box will be sufficient," Slade said. "We don't want any leftovers lying around; accidents can happen."

When he arrived at the general store to make his purchase, Thompson, the garrulous old owner, gave him his lead without any probing.

"Been quite a call for the darn stuff of late," he said. "Just a little while back a couple of fellers I never saw before bought a half dozen sticks; stowed 'em in their saddle pouches. A heck of a way to pack dynamite. Then just yesterday Pete Houck who works for the Diamond W bought two boxes. Said they aimed to blow some waterholes. Here's yours, wrapped safe. Want caps and fuse, of course?"

In a satisfied frame of mind, Slade drove back to the ranch. So the Diamond W was also buying dynamite. Of course, it could be for a perfectly legitimate purpose; Houck might have told the truth when he said it was needed to blow waterholes. That was a common enough practice. He knew that the Diamond W had hitherto refrained from using water from the irrigation creek, intimating that they too were afraid of it. Which was ridiculous on the part of a man with technical education as Rex Masters undoubtedly was. However, it tended to substantiate by seemingly tacit agreement the former belief of the cattlemen that the water could be poisoned.

Now, of course, when he, Slade, had convinced the ranchers that the water was perfectly wholesome, the logical thing for the Diamond W to do was take advantage of the water which flowed almost the entire length of their holding. The stream was small but it would fill waterholes which were needed. Yes, on the face of it, Houck's explanation of the purposed use of the explosive sounded authentic.

But Slade didn't think it was. Well, he would put it to the test, starting this very night. He could slip out of the ranchhouse in the early part of the night without arousing old Sid or the hands. Verna would have to be told, of course, but he knew he could rely on her not to talk.

She sighed when he told her what he had in mind, and her big eyes were apprehensive.

"Walt," she said, "can't you tell me who is back of the trouble that's being made? I'd feel better, dear, if you did. You know you can trust me. Can't you be like me, and holding nothing back. Can't you tell me everything?"

Slade hesitated a moment, then arrived at a decision. Another moment and she was staring wide-eyed at the star of the Rangers which he slipped from its cunningly concealed secret pocket in his broad leather waist belt.

"I'm not as surprised as I might be," she said slowly. "I've met several Rangers and there's something, perhaps a way of thought and action, that marks them. Oh, well, it might be worse. A Ranger rides a long trail, but sometimes he rides back."

"Especially if there is something very beautiful to ride back to," he replied. Verna smiled a little wistfully.

"And you will tell me who is making the trouble?"

He told her and her eyes widened with horror.

"Rex Masters and Blaine Webb!" she repeated incredulously. "My father's friends. At least he's always looked on them as his friends. And they seem so nice. Walt, are you sure?"

Point by point he laid before her his case against the pair, until she was convinced as he was.

"You must be right," she said, and shuddered. "It's terrible to think that men will do such things in the hope of gaining money."

"Some men will," he replied. "Caring nothing about

the suffering they inflict on others. The cattlemen and the farmers are pawns in the game. What happens to them means nothing just so long as it furthers their ends. Well, we shall see."

A little later he quietly got the rig on Shadow and led him from the barn. Some distance from the ranchhouse he mounted and rode swiftly north. He felt better for having confided in Verna and knew she might well be a valuable ally.

"Funny, isn't it, horse, how a man will tell things to a woman he wouldn't think of telling another man. Well, I guess it's just that woman is the greatest power in the world, at least where most of us poor men are concerned."

Shadow snorted and didn't otherwise comment.

SIXTEEN

REACHING THE VICINITY of the line of wells, Slade holed up in a thicket from which he could see and not be seen. He figured that if an attempt to blow the wells was made, it would be some time between midnight and dawn. No irreparable damage would be done, but the act would arouse the cattlemen, who would blame it on the farmers who had expressed fears that the wells would drain the lake.

The tedious hours passed, the great clock in the sky wheeled westward, and nothing happened. Slade rode back to the ranchhouse, arriving there long after full daylight. He shook his head when Verna asked if he had learned anything.

"To bed with you as soon as you eat," she said. "Dad and the boys are all out on the range; nobody will disturb you. Are you going to ride again tonight?"

"Until something happens or I conclude I'm mistaken," he replied.

The next night was a repetition of the first and Slade

began to believe that he was making a mistake. But the third night, a couple of hours after midnight, he heard the beat of horses' hoofs approaching from the south. A little later the forms of two mounted men loomed in the starlight. They dismounted near one of the wells and not more than fifty yards from the thicket in which the Ranger crouched. One fumbled something from his saddle pouch. The other led the horses off a little distance. At least the hellions didn't want the animals harmed if something should go wrong.

Together they approached the well, one carrying the bundle, the other unwinding something as he walked, apparently the length of fuse. Slade stepped from the thicket, guns ready. His voice rang out, shattering the silence—

"Elevate! You're covered!"

The two men whirled at the sound of his voice. For an instant they seemed paralyzed into inaction. Slade took a couple of steps forward. He caught a gleam of shifted metal and fired left and right. One man staggered but did not fall. Flame gushed toward the Ranger; he heard the whine of passing lead. He took quick aim and fired again; the distance was rather great for sixgun work.

There was a blinding flash, a thundering roar. Slade was knocked heels over head. He floundered on the ground, his limbs almost paralyzed by the force of the concussion. Staggering to his feet, he stood weaving, his eyes still dazzled by the flash of the explosion.

The two riderless horses were careening off across the prairie. Shadow was snorting in the thicket.

"Okay, feller, everything's under control," Slade called. He walked slowly forward, still rocking on his feet a bit.

A smoking crater was hollowed in the ground. Some distance away lay the bodies of the two men, mangled almost beyond human semblance.

"Slug hit the dynamite and it let go," he muttered. "Blazes! what a way to die!" He moved on to the bodies, bent over them and struck a match.

One's face had been completely blown away, and both

hands. The other's body was shattered but his face almost unmarred.

Going through the pockets was a grisly chore, but Slade knew he must. After considerable unpleasant fumbling with no results, he drew from the faceless man a gold watch which, marvelously, was still ticking away; he examined it carefully.

Inscribed on the back of the case were the initials, "P.H." Slade stared at them a moment.

"Well," he remarked to the watch as he carefully stowed it away, "I don't think Pete Houck will show up for work this morning." He also thought it highly unlikely that anybody would be able to identify the hideously mangled form.

The second man's face was long and white and lean. Slade recalled the description Sid Claxton gave of the man who tried to murder him in his room over the Diamond Flush. It tallied pretty well with the dead countenance before him. If the two were the same, the fellow had attempted his last drygulching.

Except for the watch, Slade replaced all the articles he had drawn forth. He straightened up, glanced at the sky. Then he made his way to the thicket where Shadow was holed up, mounted and rode south. He wished he could get a close look at the horses the unsavory pair rode, but they were nowhere in sight.

Riding at a fast pace he reached the ranchhouse before dawn and immediately went to bed and slept until the morning's activities aroused him. Verna shook her head at him when he came downstairs but said nothing.

"I'm going to ride to town," he told Claxton, who was leaving to superintend the digging of the waterholes and the preparations for the coming roundup.

"Go to it," said the rancher. "See you tonight." Slade and Verna were left alone in the living room. She gazed at him expectantly.

He told her everything. She shuddered as he described the awful death of the two dynamiters.

"And you think one of them was Pete Houck?"

"I think so, but of course I don't know for sure, having

only the initials on the watch to go by," he replied. "That's where you can lend a hand, if you will."

"I'll do anything I can, dear," she answered. "What do you want me to do?"

"Try and find out, during the next few days, if Houck is in evidence around the Diamond W," he told her. "If he isn't, the chances are the word will be handed out that he suddenly decided to quit and go elsewhere."

"I'll find out," she promised. "Do you think the other cowboys are mixed up in it?"

"I doubt it," Slade replied. "At least not the majority of them. I understand that most of them are oldtimers here who worked for the spread before it changed hands and stayed on with the new owners."

"That's right," she said. "Only Pete Houck and one or two others are new, coming here shortly after Webb and Masters purchased the ranch."

Slade nodded. Personally he was of the opinion that Pete Houck was as old in the section as he would ever be.

"I'll find out about Houck," Verna repeated. "I know some of the Diamond W boys and I'll get it out of them without them knowing that I am."

"I don't doubt it," he chuckled. "A woman can always inveigle a man into talking. Well, I'm going to ride to town and report to the sheriff."

"Going to tell him what happened?"

"Perhaps only that there are a couple of dead men on the north pasture," Slade answered. "He can draw his own conclusions."

"A good idea," Verna agreed. "I'm sure he's an honest man, but, as Dad would say, I'm afraid he was behind the door when they were handing out brains."

"Hardly that bad," Slade laughed. "But he does lack training. After all, he was just a range boss who got elected to office. Put him up against a salty bunch of his own mental calibre and you can count on him till the last brand's run."

Verna again nodded her agreement.

"Well, Shadow," Slade said as he headed for town, "at least we're thinning the sidewinders out a bit. Five altogether, now, and I don't think it is a very big outfit—eight or ten at the outside, including the pair running the show. But you're never safe with that sort of a snake till you smash the head. It grows a new body mighty fast."

Slade found the sheriff in his office. He glowered at his visitor. "What now?" he asked.

"Oh, nothing much," Slade said as he sat down, uninvited, and started rolling a cigarette. "Just a couple of gents, or what's left of them, lying by the wells on Sid Claxton's north pasture, peacefully waiting for the undertaker."

The sheriff's tilted chair legs came to the floor with a thump; he sat bolt upright, glaring.

"Not again!" he wailed. "Why did you shoot 'em?"

"I didn't," Slade replied with truth. "They were packing a load of dynamite and it exploded."

The sheriff gulped and stared. "Dynamite!" he exploded almost as loudly as the blast the night before. "What in tarnation were they doing with dynamite up there?"

"Suppose you guess," Slade suggested, touching a match to his cigarette.

"You mean," Sheriff Higgins hesitated, "you mean they aimed to blow up the wells?"

"Go to the head of the class," Slade said.

The sheriff gave a hollow groan. "Was—was it some of the—farmers?"

Slade shook his head. "No, neither of them were farmers," he replied. "One was a cowhand. The other, or I miss my guess, was a gambler or dealer, although probably he was once a cowhand."

"Did you recognize them?" asked the sheriff. Again Slade shook his black head.

"The one I have reason to believe was a cowhand had no face left—it was blown to shreds," he replied. "I doubt if his own mother, if he had one who hadn't disowned him long ago, could recognize him. The other I don't recall ever seeing before, but I have a strong notion that he was the sidewinder who drygulched Sid Claxton in his room that night and came close to killing him."

"And would have if it hadn't been for you, or so Sid says," interpolated the sheriff. "Blazes! you're a born bad luck piece. Everywhere you squat trouble just naturally sprouts."

"Maybe there won't be any after I leave," Slade observed.

"Very likely! Very likely!" the sheriff agreed heartily. He glowered at El Halcon. Then suddenly a grin split his bad tempered old face.

"Son," he said, "you 'pear to have the whole section hornswoggled, so I reckon I might as well join the procession to keep from being lonesome. No matter what you are or who you are, you've done some mighty fine chores since you landed in the section." He stuck out his gnarled hand and they shook solemnly.

"And now," Higgins suggested, "suppose you tell me about what happened last night."

Slade told him, holding back only the incident of the initialed watch and his suspicion as to its ownership.

"But why," asked the sheriff, "would anybody want to blow up those wells?"

"Remember the yarn which somebody recently started, that the wells would drain off the farmers' irrigation lake?" The sheriff nodded.

"The farmers believed that yarn, until I rode up there and talked with them and convinced them it was ridiculous nonsense," Slade said.

"You sure have a way with folks," the sheriff sighed. "Go on."

"And if the wells had been blown in and the flow of water choked off, what would the cowmen have thought?"

"That some of the farmers who believe the yarn did it," the sheriff replied without hesitation.

"Which was the general idea," Slade said. "The tension between the farmers and the cowmen would have been heightened. Get the notion?"

"Meaning that somebody is deliberately trying to stir up trouble? But in the name of tarnation, why?"

"Because somebody wants Vereda Valley," Slade answered. "If the farmers were driven away, which would very likely happen if a real rip-snorting range war cut loose, then the land could be gotten for little or nothing."

Sheriff Higgins tugged his mustache thoughtfully. "That land is valuable, now that it's irrigated," he observed.

Slade let it go at that. "But who in blazes would do such a thing?" Higgins demanded. "Do you know?"

"I have no case against anybody, yet, that would stand up in court," Slade said.

Sheriff Higgins gazed at him curiously. "You'd take a case into court?"

"I would," Slade answered. "Why not?"

"Well," the sheriff said hesitantly, "you've got a sort of—of a reputation, you know."

"Got any reward notices on me?" Slade smiled.

"No, I haven't," Higgins admitted.

"Nor has anybody else," Slade said. "I wouldn't have to worry on that score."

The sheriff shook his head and swore. "I can't make you out," he complained querulously. "But I do think that, with your ways of figuring things out, what you should be is a peace officer. What do you say, son? I can use a good deputy and with Sid Claxton's influence to back me up, I'm sure I could get the Commissioners to okay the appointment. What do you say?"

"I'll think on it," Slade promised. "The trouble is, it would sort of tie me down."

"You young fellers have always got to be gallivantin'," grumbled Higgins. "Oh, well, I did considerable when I was young and can understand how you feel. Just the same you'd be better off settling down instead of sashaying around and getting yourself a bad name and maybe getting into some real trouble 'fore you know it."

"Chances are I'll settle down, sooner or later," Slade said.

"If somebody doesn't settle your hash for you first," Sheriff Higgins predicted darkly. "I'd say right now that you've made some bad enemies in this section, if what you figure is correct. Well, I reckon I'd better get a wagon and go up and fetch those bodies in. I'll put 'em on exhibition and maybe somebody will recognize the one whose face wasn't torn up so much. Want me to keep what you told me under my hat? Looks like we've got to work together on this thing."

"Yes, I think it would be a good notion," Slade replied. He thought a moment.

"Some of the boys intended to ride up that way with a bunch of cows this morning," he said. "One of them will be sure to be tearing to town with the news. Suppose you wait until you get a report on it before you go after the bodies. What do you think?"

"I think you got the right idea," Higgins agreed. "Let folks do a mite of puzzling, especially the ones you figure are back of this hell raising. That's what we'll do."

Slade was glad that he had made peace with Sheriff Higgins and, reversing his initial intention, had to an extent confided in him. His help might come in handy. Better the situation as it was now than having him antagonistic.

SEVENTEEN

As SLADE PREDICTED, before noon a Cross C hand arrived with word of the gruesome find. With him was old Sid himself.

The sheriff at once dispatched a wagon to bring in the bodies. Claxton drew Slade aside.

"Son," he said, "I rode up there with the boys and I'm willing to bet that the one whose face wasn't cut up was the sidewinder I saw standing over me with a knife that night in the room."

"My opinion," Slade replied.

"Tell me what happened," Claxton begged. "Oh, I know you were mixed up in it somehow. What did happen, and how'd you come to catch on?"

Slade told him, again refraining to make mention of Pete Houck, for after all he was not yet sure about Houck.

The wagon with the bodies arrived at dusk. All that

evening and the following day men filed past them as they lay in the coroner's office. The faceless man was covered with a sheet, for Doc Austin ruled that there was no sense in impossing the grisly sight on people.

There was much conjecture and difference of opinion relative to the other man. Some bartenders thought his face vaguely familiar, as did a shopkeeper or two. But nobody could definitely remember having seen him or place just where.

"Nothing strange about it," Slade remarked to Claxton. "He's a quite ordinary type, the sort that drifts into a saloon, has a drink or two and ambles away without attracting any attention. He may have been in quite a few places here, but then again he may have stayed under cover in this town and found his diversion elsewhere. The important thing is that everybody agrees that he was a stranger to the section."

Claxton nodded. "Just the same a few of the boys can't help but wonder if he might have been brought in by the farmers to do the chore," he observed. "They're not saying much, but they're thinking."

"Just as some of the farmers are still not wholly convinced but that the wells will drain off their water," Slade said. "When folks are suspicious of one another, it's hard to get them to see things in the right perspective."

All of which gave Slade cause for concern. The situation was still fluid and might flow in any direction, with the two cunning devils undoubtedly working with might and main to provide the necessary impetus. It was a battle of wits between the Ranger and the unsavory pair, and Walt Slade won more fights against the outlaw brand with his wits than with his guns.

The verdict at the coroner's inquest the next day was once again typically cow country—

The two hellions were blown up by dynamite
they had no business packing where they were.
Plant 'em and forget 'em!

Verna Claxton attended the inquest, and after the verdict was rendered she mingled with various acquaintances. Later she met Slade in the lobby of the hotel.

"Well, Pete Houck suddenly decided to quit and go back to the Panhandle," she said. "Some of the Diamond W boys I talked with told me. They said Rex Masters told them last night. Guess that confirms your deduction, does it not?"

"It does," Slade replied. "You're a lucky piece."

Verna's big eyes danced and she giggled.

"Glad you think so," she said demurely.

Slade ignored this bit of byplay and repeated,

"Yes, it does, I'm glad to say. Just another link in the chain; but still nothing concrete against that pair, even could we prove the dead man is Houck, which we can't. Suppose we drop over to the Diamond Flush for a bite? Those beautiful eyes of yours might notice something I'll miss."

"I don't think your eyes miss much," she replied.

"Perhaps not, under normal conditions; but with such a distraction across the table from me, I'm not so sure."

"I think," she said, "that one of your ancestors must have kissed the Blarney Stone."

Slade chuckled. "I've heard that my great-great grandmother did," he answered. "But as I understand the situation, you must be held by the ankles, head down, to accomplish the feat; and somehow I can't see the old lady in that position."

"Doubtless she wasn't an old lady in those days, which would make a difference," Verna said. "I think I'd like to try it myself sometime, just for luck."

"Okay," he agreed. "I'll make sure you won't fall."

"Physically or metaphysically speaking?" she retorted.

"I think you should be the one to supply the answer," he replied, smiling broadly.

Verna tossed her red curls. "I think I have already supplied it," she said evenly. "Let's go eat!"

Webb and Masters were both present when they entered the saloon and sought a table. The latter appeared his normal urbane self except that his pale eyes seemed even paler than usual. Webb, on the other hand, Slade thought, was nervous, ill at ease, although he walked over to the table to greet them courteously and personally supervised their ordering.

The weak sister of the pair, Slade believed. Yes, Blaine Webb was weak, despite his saltiness and his normally assured manner. Fine when things were going smoothly, but inclined to the jitters when they were not. He believed that if the going really got rough, Webb might break. Very likely he was not nearly so hard and ruthless as he let on to be. Perhaps he was afflicted by what Slade felt pretty sure Rex Masters was not burdened with —conscience.

Yes, right now he was a quite different Webb from the Webb who so swiftly got the situation under control when he and Sid Claxton had the row the night of their first meeting.

The attempted dynamiting and the inquest were the chief topics of conversation in the saloon, which was unusually crowded for this time of day, and as Slade listened to scraps of talk that floated his way, he was inclined to agree with Claxton. There was a difference of opinion as to who might be responsible. Not that anybody came right out and accused the farmers, but the implication was plain from certain quarters. The question frequently asked, "Who else would have any reason for doing such a thing?" was not easy to answer.

Yes, the powder keg was still very much in evidence, just waiting for the match.

Verna's big eyes were everywhere. "Walt," she said abruptly, "those two men at the far end of the bar are paying us a great deal of attention."

Slade had already noticed the pair—long, lean, dangerous men with impassive countenances and watchful eyes.

"Well, can you blame them?" he bantered.

"Perhaps not, if they were paying attention to me," she conceded. "But as it happens, their attention is focused on you."

"Then they'll very likely know me if they see me again," he replied.

"Yes, that's what I'm afraid of," she returned soberly.

"I think that's exactly their intention. But you might not see them."

"Just a pair of visiting cowpokes, the chances are, who perhaps have heard of the notorious El Halcon and are giving him a once-over out of curiosity," he said lightly. Verna did not look convinced.

When they left the place after they had finished eating, old Miguel, the swamper who brought Slade warm shaving water every morning, brushed against him.

"Capitan, those two ladrones at the end of the bar," he breathed in Spanish. "Beware!"

"Si," Slade answered and passed on. Verna, who was a pace to the front, did not overhear the whispered colloquy, and Slade did not enlighten her; no sense in bothering her with the matter.

He escorted her to the hotel. "See you later," he promised. "Staying in town tonight, of course?"

"Yes, darn it!" she replied. "Doesn't really matter though—you're staying in, too." Slade chuckled and took his departure.

Leaving the hotel, he headed for his room over the Diamond Flush, where he oiled the mechanism of his guns, carefully examined the cartridges for possible flaws. Finding none, he replaced them and made sure the big Colts were working smoothly in their sheaths.

The two men, he thought, had the appearance of professional gun slingers whose guns were for hire to the highest bidder; he was familiar with the type.

Well, if it were so and they had been brought in to do a chore, it looked like the opposition was getting a bit frantic. For such men were dubious cattle to deal with. Let somebody offer them a few more pesos and they would blithely turn on their original employers. Well, he'd see; he'd outfaced that sort before. And there was always the chance, under the right conditions, that one of the sidewinders might be persuaded to do a little talking.

He returned to the hotel and he and Verna spent the rest of the afternoon and evening wandering around the town and its environs. After dinner he left her in the lobby; her eyes were dark with apprehension.

"Please be careful," she begged.

"I will, don't you worry," he promised.

"I can't help it," she replied. "I'm going to sit up late in the lobby and read, or try to. Please come to me before you go to bed."

He promised to do so. It was some time later that he entered the Diamond Flush, running his eyes over the gathering.

The two men were still at the end of the bar. More probably they had returned there after a period of absence. Slade ordered a drink and left two-thirds of it on the bar. Well, might as well get it over with. He sauntered out. In the back mirror he saw the reflections of the two men stiffen; they glanced at each other.

Slade walked slowly until he reached the corner, then quickened his pace a bit. A swift glance over his shoulder revealed the two killers walking swiftly in his wake.

What he did not see was a hunched figure stealing along in the rear of the pair, keeping at a discreet distance, in its hand something that sparkled as a beam of light struck it.

Turning the corner, Slade strode on a few paces, then turned into a small saloon frequented by cowhands. A glance showed but a scattering of patrons, including a group of a half dozen or so cowboys at the bar. One, a grizzled old waddie he recalled as attending the meeting at the Cross C ranchhouse, nodded and waved. Slade waved back, turned and faced the door. He had but a moment to wait. The swinging doors opened and the two gunmen entered, spreading out a little. Slade knew what that meant. His voice blared at them—

"Get going, you skunks!"

Hands flashed down and up. Slade shot with both guns, right and left. One man went down, blood gushing from his bullet slashed throat. The other reeled slightly but lined sights with the Ranger's breast.

But before he could pull trigger, there was a flash of light behind him. He leaped into the air, dropping his guns, shooting out his arms and legs and sprawled on his face. From between his shoulder blades protruded the handle of a heavy knife.

A hunched figure scuttled out the door and was gone; but not before Slade had recognized old Miguel, the Diamond Flush swamper. He shot a glance around the room. Nobody had moved. The cowhands at the bar did not appear particularly excited. The bartender was shaking like a leaf.

Slade holstered his guns and walked to the bar. The gray-haired waddie made room for him.

"Nice going, feller," he said. "Plumb nice going. The hellions bit off more than they could chaw. Guess they didn't know it, but they were dead men when they stepped in that door. If they'd downed you, us fellers would have filled them so full of holes they would have starved to death from leaking out their vittles. Yep, nice going, and plumb self-defense. There's seven of us fellers to swear to it. That old jigger who slipped in behind 'em did a good chore, too. A square man has friends everywhere, sometimes when he least expects them."

"Including present company," Slade replied, with a flash of his white teeth.

"You're darn right," said the cowboy. His companions nodded agreement.

"My name's Pauley, Sam Pauley," he said. "These work dodgers are—" He rattled off half a dozen names. Slade shook hands all around.

"Clyde," Pauley said to the bartender, "pour us a drink and then I reckon you better send for the sheriff and tell him to come and collect those carcasses; don't want to leave 'em there cluttering up the door. Somebody might fall over 'em and get hurt."

The barkeep managed to fill the glasses without slopping too much on the bar.

"Sorry, gents, but it's the first time I ever saw anything like that," he apologized.

"And you ain't likely to see anything just like it again, not that kind of shooting," said Pauley. "Slade, did you know those two so-and-so's?"

"Never saw them before today," the Ranger answered.

"Well, I knew one of them," Pauley said. "The one you outdrew and outshot. Called himself Shotgun Blue and claimed to have the fastest draw in Texas. Guess he was mistaken."

"Gun for hire?"

"That's right," nodded Pauley. "I can't figure how he came to be down this way; I knew him up in the Panhandle. One of those Oklahoma Border owlhoots."

Slade's eyes were thoughtful, but he did not comment.

The cook, who had discreetly remained in his cubbyhole during the shooting, was dispatched to inform the sheriff. Shortly afterward, the peace officer appeared. He glanced at the bodies, shook his head and tugged his mustache.

"Seems like all we do of late is hold inquests," he grumbled. "Well, how did all this happen."

Pauley and the others told him, profanely. The sheriff shook his head again and glanced at Slade.

"Seems you're always in the clear," he observed.

"And he always will be," Pauley said with emphasis. "Sidewinders like that blankety-blank pair ain't got no business cluttering up the earth and getting in decent folks' way."

"Guess you're right," agreed the sheriff. "Well, I'll round up some of the boys and pack the carcasses to the coroner's office."

"We'll be glad to lend you a hand," Pauley volunteered.

"Much obliged, that'll help," Higgins nodded. "Round up a couple of shutters to pack 'em on. See you tomorrow, Slade."

"We'll see you, too, if you're around," said Pauley. "Maybe you don't remember, but us fellers are from the Y-Bar-U up to the north next to the county line; we'll be in town a couple of days."

He chuckled. "Guess old Shotgun Blue was out to get himself a reputation by downing El Halcon; it didn't work," he concluded, and went in search of a shutter.

Slade did not agree with Pauley's diagnosis but refrained from saying so.

He did not accompany the grisly caravan to the coroner's office but headed for the hotel, where he found Verna sitting in the lobby, pretending to read a book.

"Thank heaven you're all right!" she exclaimed. "I was getting badly worried. I heard somebody say they heard shooting over the other side of town."

"Guess they did," Slade agreed as he sat down and began manufacturing a cigarette.

"You—saw those two men?"

"Yes, I saw them," he replied.

"And—"

"They're over at the coroner's office, what's left of them."

Verna shuddered. "Did—did you kill them?"

"I killed one," Slade admitted. "Old Miguel, the swamper at the Diamond Flush, took care of the other one, before *he* took care of me."

"I could kiss Miguel!" she declared.

"Chances are you'd scare him to death if you tried it," Slade chuckled. He thought a moment.

"I wonder," he said, "if we could persuade your father to take Miguel out to your place and let him potter around there for a while? I'm afraid if what he did should get around, something might happen to him."

"I'll answer for Dad right now," she said. "Do you think you could locate Miguel tonight?"

"I expect he's at the saloon."

"Find him and bring him here," she ordered. "We'll put him up at the hotel and he can ride with us tomorrow morning."

"I'll do that," Slade promised. "I think it's a good notion."

He pinched out his cigarette and stood up.

"And please be careful," she begged.

"I don't think there's anything more to worry about tonight," he replied and left the lobby.

Miguel was at the saloon, just finishing up his day's work.

"*Gracias, amigo,*" Slade said. "Put up your broom and mop and meet me outside."

The old Mexican asked no questions and did as he was

told. Slade escorted him to the hotel, where Verna already had a room registered for him. She thanked him for what he had done, making no mention of what it was; but Miguel understood.

He also understood the wisdom of abiding at the Cross C for a while and offered no objections when the subject was broached.

"And if I have anything to say about it, and I think I have, it will be a very long while," Verna stated definitely. Neither Miguel nor Slade argued the point with her.

"With the senorita with the hair the color of hers, it is best to agree," Miguel observed as Verna moved to the desk for a moment. "Do not you find it so, Capitan?"

"Decidedly so," Slade replied, and meant it.

"Dad's gone to bed, he was pretty well worn out," Verna said when she returned to them.

"And I'm going to follow his example," Slade said. "Had enough excitement for one day."

"I imagine one without any would be quite a novelty for you," Verna commented. "Goodnight, dear."

"Vaya usted con Dios—Go you with God," Miguel said.

EIGHTEEN

THERE WAS ANOTHER INQUEST the following afternoon. The Y-Bar-U hands in a bristling bunch were present to testify to what happened, and dare anybody to contradict them. Nobody did.

"That's old Youngman Loring's outfit, as salty as they come," Sid Claxton confided to Slade. "His range boss, Sam Pauley, could cut quite a few notches on the handle of his gun, if he was the sort to cut notches. He's the Wyatt Earp type—takes his time and never misses. If the other jigger doesn't get him on the first shot, that's all! I've heard he has a funny sliding movement from one foot to the other that throws the other jigger off balance. A good man to have with you, and a bad one to have against you."

Slade nodded agreement. He had formed something of the same estimate of Sam Pauley.

The coroner's jury wasted no time exonerating Slade and commended him for doing a good chore. It also commended the unknown gent who slipped in behind the killers and did a good chore with his sticker, 'lowing that he and Slade both were due a vote of thanks for ridding the community of the pests.

After the verdict was rendered, Sam Pauley and the Y-Bar-U bunch insisted that Slade drop in at the Diamond Flush for a drink with them.

"We don't go in there much," Pauley observed to Slade as they crossed the street. "I don't like the owner."

"Webb?"

"Oh, I don't pay him no mind," Pauley replied. "He's sort of uppity at times and sets up to be a tough, salty gent, and isn't. Step in his front door and you're out in his back yard. But the other, Masters is his name, isn't it? He's got killer eyes and ice water for blood. I don't like him. What do you think?"

"I'm inclined to agree with you," Slade admitted. In truth he was quite pleased that the shrewd old waddie had corroborated his estimate of Rex Masters. Sam Pauley had lived a long time, and he had lived a lot. Slade felt that any opinion expressed by him was worth giving serious consideration.

Rex Masters was not in evidence when they entered the saloon. Webb was at the end of the bar as usual and greeted their entrance with a cordial nod.

"You know," Sid Claxton, who had joined them, remarked contemplatively, "Blaine don't look over well to me. Face looks kind of drawn and pinched. I've a notion this business is sort of getting him down. He has most of the running of it on his hands. Masters didn't used to be around much—he handled the ranch. Of late he's been here a lot more than usual. Reckon maybe he figures Blaine may have too much to put up with. Blaine never struck me as being an indoors type. Fact is, I figure anybody who gets into the likker business needs his head looked over. Enough to drive a man loco. Always having to keep order, and trying to keep everybody happy. Ain't neither of 'em easy when the redeye is buzzin' in the ears of a passel of terrapin-brained rannies. He does a pretty good job of it, all right, but I've a notion it's sort of getting him down."

Slade was willing to agree that Blaine Webb didn't appear exactly up to snuff. His face was haggard and there was a furtive look in his dark eyes as if they were seeing things he'd rather forget. A verse of Scripture came, unbidden, to Slade's lips—"The guilty flee when no man pursueth."

Could be the case with Blaine Webb.

Listening to scraps of conversation dealing with the happenings of the night before, Slade was glad to draw the conclusion that the attempt on his life was considered a personal affair—the two gunmen out to get a reputation by downing El Halcon—and not in any way connected with the trouble between the cattlemen and the farmers. He gathered that Sam Pauley had assiduously spread the story of Shotgun Blue and his exploits along the Texas-Oklahoma Border, and very likely the yarn had lost nothing in the telling. Which, Slade felt, was all to the good. That way the incident would provide no fuel to further feed the flames. Once again his El Halcon reputation was paying off.

Soon they were surrounded by men who wanted firsthand details of the night before. Slade let Sam Pauley supply them, which the Y-Bar-U range boss did with gusto. Slade received approving nods from all sides.

"Gave 'em their comeuppance proper, eh, son?" chortled old Bass Hogadorn. "Fine chore! Fine chore! We don't want that kind of cattle maverickin' into our section. We got the best of everything here. Including our badmen," he added with a creakly chuckle.

A roar of laughter greeted the sally.

"Let's all have a drink on it," said Hogadorn. He raised his glass solemnly to Slade; but there was a twinkle in his faded eyes.

Once again Walt Slade asked himself the question, "What next?" He suffered no illusion that the abortive attempt on his life by the two imported gunmen would be the last try. The resourceful hellions would think of something else, and without delay. They appeared able to make capital of anything; even drilling the artesian wells had provided them with an unforeseen opportunity to start a row. Very quickly, he was convinced, they would cut loose somewhere, and no doubt with something novel.

Thus he meditated as he and old Sid rode home under the stars. The rancher was mostly silent, but presently he chuckled a little.

"Old Bass is hard to beat," he remarked apropos of the redoubtable Hogadorn. "He manages to see something funny in everything; but he's shrewd and doesn't miss any bets. He told me privately that he didn't take any stock in the notion that those two sidewinders were just out to get a reputation. He said in his opinion they were brought in deliberately by somebody to kill you. Said you are in somebody's way and it won't be the last try at getting rid of you. I asked him if he had any notion who that somebody could be. He sort of screwed up his face and his eyes looked funny. He said,

" 'Folks will likely be mighty surprised when they find out.' Then he stopped a minute, seemed to be making up his mind about something and said, 'Slade knows.' That was all I could get out of him."

"That was enough," the Ranger replied, his eyes thoughtful. He believed Hogadorn could make a pretty accurate guess as to just who was responsible and hoped he wouldn't do any loose talking. He was pretty well convinced, however, that the old fellow didn't know why somebody was so anxious to eliminate him. Claxton seemed to read his thoughts, to an extent, for as they rode into the ranchhouse yard, he remarked,

"Bass don't talk. What he told me won't go any farther; we're old *amigos* and we're both interested in you, that's all."

Working for Claxton as he was, nominally, at least,

Slade made it his business to keep a close watch on the waterholes, the overflow from the wells and, more especially, the small stream which was the residue of the farmers' irrigation project. He didn't put much stock in the contaminated water. In his opinion the cows had died from eating water hemlock, which grows along the bank of small streams and irrigation ditches, and sometimes, though not often, around waterholes.

Cattle are very fond of water hemlock. They will even wade far out into a stream or actually kneel down on the banks to reach it below them. And within a few hours the animals that partake of it are rigid. The description of the poisoned animals in the section tallied more with water hemlock poisoning than the results of arsenic or strychnine. He had warned Claxton that the irrigation stream might well be favorable to wild parsnip, as the cowmen called the plant, and had advised frequent inspection of the waterholes and the stream.

"The darned stuff can be rooted out and controlled if you don't let it get the jump on you," he told the rancher, and proceeded to keep a sharp eye out for the lethal plant.

"Looks like even Nature plays into the hands of those two rapscallions," he wryly remarked to Shadow in the course of one of their rides.

As was his wont, he familiarized himself with the terrain, especially near the western hill slopes, and quickly discovered that the old trail which ultimately turned westward through the hills, the Vereda Trail, was much the shorter route into Vereda Valley. Bypassing the town, it skirted the base of the hills. The main trail to the north often trended eastward in sweeping curves to tap the various ranches, while the Vereda followed a direct course to the south before turning into the valley. He stowed this knowledge in the back of his mind for possible future reference. Eventually he was glad that he did.

In the southwest Texas country there comes at times, especially in the fall, a series of days of exquisite beauty. When the air is soft and balmy and so still that no leaf moves. When the rangeland is flooded with golden sunshine, the grass heads tipped with glowing amethyst fire, the hill tops veiled in a mystic violet haze. All is sunshine and peace and quiet loveliness that begets a feeling of well being.

But oldtimers have learned to look upon such days with suspicion. All too often they are harbingers of trouble. Gradually the deep blue of the sky is tarnished by a creeping gray. A little wind breathes up from the southwest, lulls, blows a trifle harder, ceases altogether. Now the sky is slatey with flecks of ragged cloud hurrying across the darkening arch. Men hold their breath in dread anticipation, and wait. Usually they don't have long to wait. The wind blows again, fitfully, from the southeast. Follows a period of utter calm. Then down from the flattop mountains of New Mexico roars a mighty tempest with hail and lightning and dishing rain. Tragedy may well stalk naked through the land. At the very best, dire discomfort and danger can be expected, and usually do not disappoint.

During the days that followed, peaceful, quiet, with no untoward incident, Walt Slade began to develop an uneasiness akin to that of waiting for the storm to break. Nothing untoward happened, nor were there any signs that something was going to happen. Masters and even Webb appeared serene and free from apprehension. The ranchers were going about their business cheerfully, likewise the farmers. On the surface it appeared that real peace had descended, and to stay.

However, Slade was not fooled by these placid surface indications. Not for a moment did he believe that the two schemers had given up, far from it. He was positive they were cooking up something and bent every effort to forestall it, whatever it might be.

He took to riding the hills to the west, for he still believed them the focal point of whatever the pair had in mind. Even the hills appeared peaceful for a change, benign in the bright sunshine, but Slade had a feeling that they were only waiting.

One day he was riding a chunky bay that was a good rock horse but not noted for speed. Shadow had bruised an ankle and needed a day or two of rest. Far up in the hills, on an offshoot of the main trail, by which the crest of the rock wall surrounding the lake could be reached, he suddenly pulled his mount to a halt. Somewhere behind on the twisting track was a faint clicking, the sound of a horse's irons. Could be just one of the farmers looking things over, of course, but it could be someone else. Slade backed the bay into a dense thicket, from where he could see and not be seen, and waited. A few minutes later a rider mounted on a fine big moros swung around the bend and into view. He was a rather tall man with broad shoulders. His face, indistinct in the shadow of his low-drawn hatbrim, was unknown to the Ranger. Perhaps just a chuck line riding cowhand taking a short cut to the northwest; very likely was.

Just the same, Slade, after waiting until he had passed around the next bend to the west and the sound of his passing dimmed to silence, sent the bay trailing in the same direction. He rode cautiously, for it was best not to take chances in this blasted section. Once he spotted the lone rider just topping a distant rise which was not far from the wall crest. He quickened the bay's pace, shoved him close against the shadowy growth and pulled to a halt on the crest of the rise. Now he had a clear view of the track ahead, which wound up to the top of the wall, following one of the few rideable slants to the summit. For a moment the horseman stood out hard and clear against the sky as he reached the crest, then faded from view after turning south along the rock parapet. Slade hesitated a moment, rode on.

Half way up the slope was a bristle of thicket. When he reached it, he dismounted and concealed the bay in its depths. Then, consumed by curiosity, he cautiously mounted the remainder of the steep slant on foot, until he could peer over the outer edge of the parapet. He found he was not far from the south wall of the cup, and quickly spotted his quarry.

The fellow had dismounted, leaving his horse standing, and was walking slowly along the summit of the south wall. To all appearances he had lost something and was hunting for it, for his eyes were fixed on the ground searchingly. From time to time he would pause and stand apparently in thought. Twice he lay down on his stomach and peered over the outer edge of the wall. Then he resumed his slow pacing, peering at the rock surface, pausing, moving on, pausing again.

Slade knew that the man was out of sight of the shack which housed the flume guards. And due to the configuration of the slope which ran down to the cliff crests he could not be seen from the valley floor. Facts of which he was evidently aware for he showed no signs of apprehension and his movements were not in the least furtive.

But what the devil was he up to! What was the meaning of that seemingly aimless pacing? What did he expect to find? Slade hadn't the slightest idea and nothing developed to give him a hint as to what the fellow might have in mind.

Finally the apparently unrewarded searcher gave it up, whatever it was. He turned abruptly and walked back to where he had left his horse on the east wall, with purposeful steps. Slade slid from view and hurried back down the slope to the thicket. He had barely reached his place of concealment when he heard the clatter of the moros' hoofs on the slope above. Hoping to get a glimpse of the fellow's face, he slid to the edge of the growth and stood motionless behind a final straggle of brush.

The rider came into view, travelling at a good pace; Slade leaned forward, peering intently. And just as the horseman was opposite where he stood, the bay sneezed prodigiously.

The mounted man whirled, jerked a gun, fired twice in the direction of the sound and drove his spurs home. Slade felt the wind of the passing slugs. Wrathfully he whipped his own guns from their sheaths and cut down on the hellion as he swerved around the next bend. The fellow reeled in the saddle but kept his seat and kept going like the wind. Quickly the beat of his horse's irons dimmed into the distance.

Ejecting the spent shells from his guns and replacing them with fresh cartridges, Slade walked to his horse and

mounted. No sense in trying to run the devil down; the
bay wouldn't have a chance against the big moros.

"Blast it! Why couldn't I have been forking Shadow
today?" Slade muttered as the bay pushed his way through
the growth to the trail. Well, nothing was to be gained
by crying over it.

"Not your fault, horse," he told the bay. "Guess when a
critter has to sneeze he has to sneeze, and nobody told you
we might eat lead as a result. Didn't figure on it myself;
seems I keep getting more careless as the days go by.
Should have known that horned toad was up to something
he wouldn't want spotted. Well, by pulling his iron he
told me it was something that wouldn't stand the light
of day; but what? His actions didn't seem to make sense,
but then nothing seems to make sense in this confounded
section. Let's go, horse, I'm hungry."

In no very good temper and with his curiosity unas-
suaged, he rode back to the Cross C ranchhouse.

The puzzling incident was important in the light of
subsequent developments, and had Slade been able to
read the riddle aright, much trouble could well have been
averted.

Three days later the blowup came. Verna was visiting
at a neighboring ranchhouse. Old Sid was out on the range
looking things over preparatory to the roundup. The hands
were busy around the ranchhouse at various chores. Some
were putting new shingles on the barn. Others were
straightening corral posts and stringing wire. Still others
were in the blacksmith shop hammering out horse shoes
and other metal parts.

But when Slade rode in from the north pasture shortly
before noon, there was nobody in sight save old Miguel
who was standing in the door as if awaiting him.

"Where is everybody?" Slade asked.

"Capitan," replied Miguel, "there is trouble. Less than
an hour before a vaquero rode in with word that the
farmers are marching from the valley to destroy the ranchers. The Senor Yates, the range boss, ordered the men to

mount their *caballos* at once. They rode, most swiftly, to stop the farmers."

"The devil you say!" Slade exclaimed. "What became of the fellow who brought the word?"

"He rode north, to warn the other ranchers, or so he said," Miguel answered.

"Yes, so he said," Slade remarked grimly. "Listen, Miguel, when the Senor Claxton arrives, tell him what you just told me. And tell him I've ridden to get ahead of those loco jugheads and stop this foolishness. Got it straight, now? Don't forget. I've got to cut that bunch off before they reach the valley. Be seeing you."

"*Capitan*, they rode swiftly," Miguel called after him as Shadow got under way.

"But not swiftly enough," Slade flung back at him. "Trail, Shadow, trail! Tell the *patron* as soon as he arrives, Miguel."

As a matter of fact, old Sid reached the ranchhouse only a few minutes after Slade departed.

At a fast and even faster pace, Slade sent the great black horse on a long diagonal to the southwest to reach the Vereda Trail. In a surprisingly short time he reached it and Shadow's hoofs rang on the hard surface as he proceeded to give the very best that was in him, which was plenty.

Slade estimated the distance the informal posse must have covered, allowing for the fact that their gait must be governed by the speed of the slowest horse. He was fairly sanguine in his hope to reach the valley mouth ahead of them, and when the trail swerved into the great depression between the hills he was confident that he was in front. Another mile or so and he received evidence that he was. Around a brush flanked bend and directly ahead was a low ridge paralleling the trail, and as he drew near, a score of heads came into view. The farmers, some of them, were holed up waiting.

Once before Slade had faced a similar situation, and had handled it, with a little help from an unexpected source. He pulled Shadow to a halt and faced the embattled farmers.

"Well, what's the big notion?" he demanded.

"Slade," replied old Lije Bixby, "the cattle fellers are riding this way to clean out the valley. A feller rode in a little while back and warned us they were coming. We're ready for them. Might as well get this thing over once for all."

"There's nobody riding this way except a bunch of loco rannies who fell for the same lie you fellows fell for," Slade said. "Their informant told them you fellows were riding to town to clean out the ranchers. Neither of you had the brains to investigate a little before going off half-cocked. All right, come out of that and line up in the trail behind me. I'll handle this situation. Don't one of you make a move when those addle-pated cowboys show up. I'll handle them."

The farmers, albeit somewhat reluctantly and looking dubious, obeyed him. They left the shelter of the ridge and spread apart across the trail, rifles at the ready. Slade rolled a cigarette, leaned against a tree and waited, some two hundred yards in front of the farmers, too far for accurate six-gun work.

He had quite a little while to wait and was finishing his second cigarette when the drumming of hoofs announced the arrival of the Cross C hands. They bulged around the bend, saw Slade standing in the middle of the trail and jolted to a halt.

They also saw that they were distinctly at a disadvantage against the farmers' rifles and dismounted quickly, spreading out in open order.

Slade watched them, smoking calmly, until they started to advance, slowly and cautiously. He waited until they had covered a few paces, then held up his hand.

"Hold it!" he said. "That's far enough."

The cowboys halted, glowering. Clem Yates, his face distorted by anger, spoke.

"Listen, Slade," he said, "we like you, but we're going to have it out with these skunks and you're not going to stop us."

"Think not?" Slade replied composedly, pinching out the butt of his cigarette and casting it aside.

"No, you're not," Yates repeated. "We don't want to do you in, but we will if you don't get out of the way. What's the matter with you, anyhow? Have you gone loco? There's fifty of us to your one. We can kill you, and we will, if you make us."

"Oh, I reckon you can kill me, all right, there's certainly enough of you to do the chore," Slade answered. "But, Clem, you and five or six others won't live to see it done." His hands flashed down and up, the black muzzles of his Colts yawned at Yates.

"All right, Clem, ready to start fanging?" he asked, his voice musical, friendly. "If so, get going and make your play."

Clem Yates shifted from one foot to the other. His face darkened, his hands twitched; he hesitated.

So did his companions. The issue was plain. Slade had thrown down the gauntlet and it was up to them to decide. He was ready to die, if necessary. Were they? Sure they could kill him—fifty to one. A single well-directed shot would do it. But how many would go down before those blazing guns dropped from his stiffened hands? Each man present had an unpleasant premonition that he was singled out for personal attention. Fifty to one! Still—they hesitated.

NINETEEN

But SLADE KNEW THE SITUATION was packed with dynamite. The cowboys had their bristles up. Behind him the farmers were ready with their rifles. A misinterpreted move on the part of somebody would set off the explosion. Regretfully, he opened his lips to peal forth the words that would give pause to any gathering between the Red River and the Rio Grande—

"In the name of the State of Texas! Under the authority of the Texas Rangers—"

A clatter of hoofs sounded. Around the bend galloped

a foam flecked roan horse. And forking that horse was the maddest man Walt Slade had ever seen. The Cross C hands seemed suddenly smitten by perturbation.

Sid Claxton left the saddle with his horse in full stride. He rocked on his heels, caught his balance and plowed straight for Clem Yates.

"You!" he roared. "What do you mean by starting a rukus without getting my permission?"

"Boss, we thought—" Yates began.

"You thought!" howled Claxton. "You never had a thought in your empty skulls! I'll thought you!"

He made a rush for Yates, who turned to run, but not quickly enough. Claxton's Number Twelve boot caught him solidly in the seat of the pants. With a bellow of woe he sailed through the air to thud on his face in the dust. Old Sid sideswiped another hand with his huge paw and sent him spinning through the air to land squarely on top of Clem Yates, who was struggling to rise. Yates flattened out with a strangled squawk and bleated for mercy. The other Cross C hands were in full flight to escape the foot and hand of their irate boss. Claxton charged at Yates, who scuttled away on all fours to join the rout of horses careening around the bend. Old Sid shook his fist and volleyed profanity after them.

Walt Slade leaned against a convenient tree and laughed till he had to hang onto the trunk for support. Claxton shot him an indignant glance and turned on the farmers.

"And you!" he bawled. "What do you mean by sashaying down here looking for trouble? Ain't there enough fatherless kids hereabouts without you adding to their number? Get the blankety-blank back to your crops and let's not have any more of this blankety-blank foolishness!"

Looking sheepish, the farmers melted away. Weak from laughter, Slade managed to mount his horse. Old Sid followed suit, rumbling and muttering.

"I told 'em!" he growled. "A pity I ain't a mite younger —I'd have caught me more of the blankety-blank terrapin-brained wind spiders. I've stood all of this nonsense I'm going to stand."

"You showed up at a mighty good time, sir," Slade chuckled. "You turned into a comedy what might well have ended a tragedy. You made the whole crowd, both sides, look silly, and that will have a more lasting effect than facing them down with guns."

"But if you hadn't gotten here first I'd have been too late," said Claxton. "And," he added, "I've a notion you had things pretty well under control already."

"Perhaps," Slade conceded, "but it was a ticklish stituation. I ran up against a somewhat similar one once before, and it ended in much the same way," he observed, with a reminiscent chuckle.

"Clem Yates is a good range boss and a good cowman, but he sure was down in the basement when they were handing out brains. Falling for a yarn like that!" Claxton snorted.

"It must have been very smoothly handled," Slade defended Yates' implied lack of cerebral functioning. "Remember, the farmers fell for it, too, and they're a hardheaded lot. When folks are suspicious of one another they are always too ready to arrive at conclusions that favor their way of thinking. It's one of the oldest and most effective owlhoot tricks—set two factions against each other, with each blaming the other for anything that happens."

Claxton suddenly turned to face him. "Slade," he said, "do you know who is back of this heck raising?"

"Yes," Slade replied wearily. "Yes, I know, but I can't prove it."

"To the devil with proving it!" growled Claxton. "Let's go gun the horned toads and get it over with."

Slade shook his head. "Taking the law in your own hands is bad business, especially when you have no proof with which to back up your actions," he replied. "I wonder sometimes, though," he continued gloomily. "If those hellions are allowed to run around loose, more men may die. It came very near happening today. If I hadn't arrived at the ranchhouse when I did, the two bunches would very likely have tangled and the whole section would have been embroiled."

"You're darn right," Claxton grunted. "I figure it was touch-and-go for a while."

"Yes, but I've a notion it will be a lot harder to start a row after today," Slade obeserved. "You made a lot of friends in the valley today, Mr. Claxton."

Old Sid grinned. "Funny way to make friends," he said. "Bawl the heck outa them."

"But your attitude showed plainly that you had their welfare at heart," Slade pointed out. "They noted it, and they won't forget."

"I hope not," said Claxton. "Things are sure a sight better than when you coiled your twine here, despite what's been happening. You deserve a lot of credit, son. Oh, heck, let's hustle to town and get that drink; I feel in need of it."

There were quite a few cowhands and some owners in the Diamond Flush when they entered, but the Cross C waddies were conspicuous by their absence.

"And they'd better stay absent for a while," growled Claxton. "I'm still in the notion of larrupin' a few more of the terrapin-brains."

Men came over to talk with Claxton and Slade, word of the near encounter having gotten around. They shook their heads and cast admiring glances at Slade as old Sid graphically described what had happened.

"And if I can get my hands on those horned toads who put out those infernal lies, when I get through with them, folks won't be able to tell them from a fresh hide," he declared.

After a bit, Slade slipped out for a while, leaving Claxton and the others still discussing the event. As he sauntered along the street, he met Jethro Persinger and Nate. The farmers greeted him warmly.

"We heard about what was going on too late to get there," said Jethro. "We might have been able to hammer some sense into those addlepates. Everything worked out okay, though, thanks to you and Mr. Claxton." He chuckled. "Lije Bixby said he never got such a talking to as Mr. Claxton handed 'em, but that it plumb made sense. Won't be easy for anybody to start something like that again. The boys are out looking for that feller who stirred 'em up with his lies."

"Highly unlikely that they'll find him," Slade commented. "I imagine he kept right on going after spreading the false rumor. The same goes for the one who got the Cross C hands riled. He said he was riding north to warn the other ranchers, but you can bet he never stopped at another spread."

Suddenly Slade had an inspiration. "Tell you what," he said, "Mr. Claxton is in the Diamond Flush. Suppose you drop in with me and pass the time of day. I've an idea he'll be glad to see you."

"Well, if you think so, I reckon it's a good idea," admitted Jethro.

There were stares when Slade entered in company with the Persingers, but old Sid rose to the occasion without ruffling a feather. He shook hands with the Persingers and invited them to have a drink.

"From Kentucky, eh?" he remarked by way of making conversation. "What part?"

"Grayson county," Jethro told him.

"Hmmm!" said Claxton. "Happen to run into any Coys over there? They're distant relations of mine, on my mom's side."

"Why, yes, quite a few," replied Jethro. He rattled off a string of names. Claxton nodded.

"I heard Mom talk about 'em," he observed. "The only one I ever met was old Cynthia Coy, who visited us once; she lived nigh onto a hundred."

"One of her boys is a judge, the other a banker, nice folks," Jethro instantly replied.

An animated discussion followed, with a naming of names and a tracing of lineage. Claxton turned to young Nate.

"Slade tells me you hanker to be an engineer," he remarked.

"That's right, Mr. Claxton," Nate answered shyly.

"Hmmm!" said old Sid, his eyes thoughtful. Slade suppressed a smile.

"This has been mighty interesting," Claxton said as the

Persingers prepared to go. "Tell you what, suppose you boys drop over to my place when you find time and we'll have another gab about Kentucky folks. Okay?"

"We'll be glad to, Mr. Claxton," Jethro accepted. "Yes, it's been a nice talk. Much obliged for everything."

The Persingers took their leaves; Claxton followed them to the door with his eyes.

"Nice people," he commented. "And that boy strikes me as being up-and-coming."

"He is," Slade said. "I predict the world will hear about him some day."

"Wouldn't be surprised if you're right," nodded old Sid, his eyes still thoughtful.

Claxton decided he'd like to look at a few hands in a nearby poker game. Slade left the Diamond Flush and resumed his interrupted walk. He was passing a small saloon on Worth Street when he heard a voice calling his name. Glancing around, he saw Clem Yates poke his head out the door and peer cautiously up and down the street.

"Slade," he said, "I'm plumb sorry for what happened. Really I am. Reckon a feller just has to make a darn fool of himself now and then. Do you think you could sort of make peace for us with the Old Man?"

"I'm pretty sure I can," Slade replied, smiling broadly, "but I'd advise you to steer clear of him for a while. He's still in no very good temper."

"You're darned right I will," Yates replied, giving his posterior portions a reminiscent rub.

"I think he'll get over his mad before long," Slade comforted the range boss. "By the way, Clem, did you know the man who brought you that lie?"

Yates shook his head. "Never saw him before," he replied. "He said he aimed to sign up with a spread here, that he passed through the valley and saw what the farmers were up to and figured the cowmen ought to know about it."

"And you never thought to stop in town and check on his story?"

"No, we didn't," Yates admitted sheepishly. "We hollered to a few fellers we knew and kept on riding; figured we didn't have any time to waste."

Slade shook his head, and wondered if old Sid might have the right of it relative to Clem's lack of gray matter.

"Try and not be taken in by another such yarn," Slade advised. "Yes, I'll try and square things with the Old Man." He passed on, leaving Yates looking considerably relieved.

Slade strolled about the town for a couple of hours. Then he sat in the hotel lobby, smoking and thinking. Dusk was falling when he returned to the Diamond Flush in quest of something to eat.

Old Sid was still playing poker. Webb and Rex Masters were not in evidence, the head bartender being in charge. Slade wondered where the two miscreants might be, and what new deviltry they were cooking up. Doubtless they had already been informed of the valley debacle and were trying to evolve something with which to counteract its effects.

TWENTY

At that moment Blaine Webb was nervously pacing the floor of the Diamond W ranchhouse living room. Rex Masters sat at a table watching him, a contemplative look in his pale eyes. Nearby two hard-faced individuals lounged in chairs, smoking. Webb spoke.

"In my opinion the best thing we can do is forget the whole infernal business," he said. "We're doing all right here, legitimately. If we don't drop it, we'll end losing everything, and lucky if we aren't pushing up the daisies. You can't kill him, you can't stop him. He outsmarts us at every turn."

"I consider he's overrated," Masters replied. "He's just managed to get some lucky breaks, that's all."

"I suppose out-drawing Shotgun Blue and plugging him through the neck was just a lucky break," Webb observed sarcastically.

"He did get a lucky break there," Masters said. "Gulden would have downed him if old Miguel—oh, it was Miguel, all right—hadn't stuck a knife in his back before he could pull trigger."

Webb did not look at all impressed and continued his jerky pacing.

"Sometimes I don't think the hellion is human," he growled. "Even blowing down a cliff on top of his head didn't faze him. And he's always one jump ahead of us. Look at what happened to Houck and Blundel up by the artesian wells! Somehow he managed to blow them both to Hades with their own dynamite. Oh, he was mixed up in it somehow, no doubt in my mind as to that."

"They were a couple of bunglers and very likely blew up themselves," said Masters. "And as for the cliff—there was more bungling. Bad timing was all; I should have handled that chore in person."

"No matter what else Blundel was, he was a good powder man, as you very well know," Webb differed. "He didn't bungle the chore; Slade was just too blasted smart for him, on that I'm willing to wager."

"The terrible El Halcon has got you buffaloed," Masters sneered.

"I'm not buffaloed," Webb denied flatly. "It's just that I've got the sense to recognize the patent fact when I'm outclassed. I wouldn't have a chance with him with a gun, and I know it. And he thinks as fast as he shoots, which is something you'd better give a little thought to. He's gotten the farmers and the cowmen together, something nobody would have believed possible. And after today's blunder there isn't a chance in the world to get them on the prod against each other again. He's got Sid Claxton hogtied; and the sheriff, too. You're supposed to be the brains of this outfit; you'd better start using them. And I still think the sensible thing would be to forget the blasted stuff while we're in one piece."

"I don't intend to pass up a million dollars because of a few difficulties," Masters said coldly. "And as for brains—I've been using mine. I've got a nice little plan worked out that will accomplish our ends despite Senor Slade. Now listen."

He lowered his voice and talked earnestly for a few minutes. As the plan unfolded, Blaine Webb's eyes widened and an expression of horror fleeted across his face.

"Rex," he protested, "it would be wholesale murder!"

Masters shrugged his broad shoulders. "A few more won't matter," he said. "We're in as deep as we can get right now. They can only hang you once."

Webb did not reply. He walked to the window and stood staring out into the night, his fingers twitching. Masters gazed at him reflectively, turned to the two men lounging in the chairs and nodded. The pair nodded back with what was apparently understanding and agreement.

Slade enjoyed a leisurely dinner and then sat comfortable and relaxed, reviewing recent incidents through the blue haze of his cigarette. He felt quite good about the day's developments. Of one thing he was now convinced, a very important one thing, there would be no range war in the section. The sheer absurdity of the bungled attempt to stir up trouble, and its comic ending, had impressed both cowmen and farmers to a greater extent than would have some grim and dramatic happening. Men don't like to be laughed at, especially when the laughter is inspired by their own foolishness. Both sides felt they had been thoroughly duped; which registered a bond of sympathy.

Now it would appear his only chore was to drop a loop on the pair responsible for all the trouble. Appeared to be something of a chore, all right, but with peace and good feeling replacing a war of nerves and enmity, the difficulty shouldn't be insurmountable. He felt that he had Webb and Masters on the run and too busy trying to cover their own tracks to have time for cooking up some more skulduggery.

In which he decidedly underestimated Rex Masters' capacity for sheer hellishness, his tenacity of purpose and his devilish ingenuity. In other words, with his back to the wall, Rex Masters was at his best.

Also, another factor which played into Masters' hands—

the farmers were lulled into a sense of false security. With peace made with the cattlemen, they felt they had little more to fear. In which they were as wrong as Slade's estimate of the situation. Afterward, he wondered how he could have arrived at so erroneous a conclusion. Oh, well, as Clem Yates said, a fellow just has to make a darn fool of himself now and then. Evidently even a Texas Ranger was no exception.

Old Sid cashed in his chips and clumped over to Slade's table. "What say, suppose we go home," he suggested. "I'm ready to call it a night."

Several uneventful days followed. The Persingers, father and son, visited the Cross C and were cordially received. Even by a subdued Clem Yates, who went out of his way to be nice to them.

Verna and young Nate appeared to find a good deal in common, a development Slade noted with pleasure.

He and Verna rode to town a day or two later, the girl wishing to make some purchases. They ate dinner at the Diamond Flush. Neither Webb nor Masters were in evidence, but Slade noticed that the Diamond Flush hands were present in a body. Evidently they had been given a night off prior to the busy days of preparation for the coming beef roundup.

It was late when Slade and the girl headed for home through a very beautiful night. There was a brilliant moon in the sky and the prairie was aglow with silver radiance. Every twig and branch of the thickets was tipped with the pale glitter and the great hush charmed them to silence.

When they passed the Diamond W ranchhouse there was a light burning in the living room. Apparently Webb and Masters were spending the night at home.

They rode on, climbed a shallow rise and reached its crest, which was dark in the shadow cast by a tall growth flanking the trail.

Suddenly there was the sound of a single gunshot somewhere behind them, a muffled sound as if the arm had been fired indoors. Slade pulled up quickly and they sat gazing back the way they had come.

"Now what in blazes was that?" the Ranger wondered,

staring at the distant loom of the Diamond W ranchhouse, every detail of which was plain in the flood of moonlight.

As they gazed, the front door opened and three men came out, paused a moment, then hurried to the barn. A few minutes later they reappeared, mounted, and rode swiftly west by north. Slade watched them grow small in the distance, his black brows drawing together.

"Something funny about all this," he told his companion. "Of course it could just have been somebody letting off a shot by accident while cleaning a gun or something."

He continued to gaze at the silent building with the one glowing window, arrived at a decision.

"You stay here," he ordered the girl. "I'm going to have a closer look."

She didn't answer, but Slade took it for granted she'd remain where he told her to. He turned Shadow and rode swiftly back down the slope. A hundred yards or so from the building he dismounted, leaving the horse invisible in the shadow of a straggle of thicket. With quick lithe steps he made his way to the ranchhouse, paused to listen a moment, then silently mounted the veranda steps. Crossing the porch, he peered through the window, and uttered a sharp exclamation.

A man lay on the floor of the living room, motionless. The beams from a lamp fell full on his face and Slade recognized Blaine Webb.

Slade crossed to the door, opened it and stepped into the room. After a quick glance around, he knelt beside the prostrate man. Webb was still alive but unconscious and breathing in stertorous gasps. He had been shot through the chest. Slade opened his shirt and gazed at the small blue hole a little above the location of the heart. There was very little blood showing, but from the wound a frothy bubble rose and fell. The Ranger knew what that meant—a wind wound, internal bleeding. He looked up quickly at the sound of a step on the veranda.

Verna stood in the door, her eyes wide, horror filled. "I had to come, I was afraid something would happen to you," she said, her voice little above a whisper. "The house looked so terrible, so silent and lonely. Is—is he dead?"

Slade shook his head. "Not yet, but I'm afraid he won't last long," he replied. "Filling up inside, I'd say. There's nothing I can do for him." He hesitated a moment.

"Verna," he said. "I'll stay here with him while you ride to town and fetch Doctor Austin. It's only about four miles and you should make it there and back in an hour. Perhaps Doc can do something for him, although I doubt it. But he might be able to bring him back to consciousness before he takes the Big Jump. Then perhaps he could tell us what happened. Something very strange about this."

"But those men we saw ride away from here—what if they should come back?" Verna said.

"I don't think there's any cause to worry about them," Slade replied. "I imagine it will be quite a while before they put in an appearance; they rode away on some definite chore, unless I'm greatly mistaken. I'm very anxious to learn, if possible, what that chore is. Get going, honey."

The girl hesitated no longer. A moment later the clatter of her horse's hoofs dimmed away in the distance. Slade did not dare move the wonded man. He sat down in a nearby chair and waited. Webb continued to breathe in short gasps, but for the present there appeared to be no change in his condition.

It was a long wait. Considerably more than an hour elapsed before the sound of hoofs heralded Verna's return with the doctor.

Doc Austin hurried into the room, nodded to Slade and at once began his examination. He straightened up, shook his head.

"Only a matter of minutes," he said. "Massive internal bleeding. No time for an operation, even if one would help, which is highly improbable. There's nothing I can do."

"Doc," Slade said, "do you think you could cause him to regain consciousness, if only for a minute or two before he dies? There are some questions I'm very anxious to ask him."

"I'll try," Austin replied. "A heart stimulant may do the trick. Dying men have a habit of regaining consciousness with their mind clear for a short period before death. I'll try."

He opened his satchel, secured a hypodermic.

Swiftly, but with the greatest care he charged it. "Too much of a dose might cause him to go off at once," he muttered. "There, I think that should do it if anything will."

He inserted the needle, drove the plunger home. "Now we can only wait, and hope," he said.

The minutes dragged past, and to Walt Slade each seemed an eternity. He had a terrible premonition that something frightful was due to happen. And just what only Blaine Webb could tell him. He could see no change in the livid, distorted face of the dying man. Only, it seemed to him, Webb's breathing had accelerated a trifle. Then he realized that his eyelids were fluttering.

"Coming out of it," said Doc. "You'll have to work fast —he has mightly little time."

Webb's eyes opened, blankly. He stared into Slade's face with no sign of recognition; then abruptly his expression changed.

"He shot me," he breathed through his blood frothing lips. "We quarrelled over it and he shot me."

Slade bent closer. "Webb," he said tensely. "Can you hear me?"

"Yes," the other whispered.

"Webb, who shot you, and why?" the Ranger asked.

"Masters," Webb faltered. "I couldn't go along with him and help him send all those poor people to death— I couldn't. I tried to make him stop—and he killed me."

"What is it he's going to do?" Slade urged.

Webb seemed to rally a little, his eyes brightened under the film that was drifting across them.

"Slade!" he breathed. "Maybe you can get there in time to stop him. He's going to blow the retaining wall and let the lake into the valley. No guards at the flume any more. He's a mining engineer and knows how to do it. Everybody in the valley will be drowned. Try—and—stop him—Slade! Promise!"

"I promise," the Ranger replied.

"Did—did bad things—but—but that was—too—much. Couldn't—do it. Stop him—Slade."

"I will," Slade replied. "And I think you've made up for everything you've done that wasn't just right."

The shadow of a smile touched the dying man's lips. "I—hope—so," he breathed. His eyes closed wearily, and did not open again.

Doc Austin felt his heart. "He's gone," he said quietly.

Slade stood up, his face set in granite lines. "Verna," he said, "you will ride for the valley as fast as your horse will take you and warn everybody of their danger. Stop at the Persingers' place first and enlist their aid. The folks farther up the valley will be in the most danger. Herd them up the west slopes where they'll be safe. Don't let them stop to take anything along. There may not be a minute to spare. And keep as close to the slopes as you can."

"And you?" the girl asked quietly.

"I'm riding to the lake," he replied. "Maybe I can get there in time to stop him; I'll try. Doc, will you ride on to the Cross C and tell Claxton and his boys to ride for the valley to help if they can? Okay. Come on, Verna, let's go!

"Don't push your horse till he gets into his full stride," he admonished her as they mounted. "Ride south by west till you hit the old Vereda Trail and follow it into the valley; it's the shortest route. And keep as close to the west slopes as you can," he repeated. "Hasta luego—till we meet again."

"I hope," she replied. "Please try to be careful, dear." She rode off, tears streaming down her face.

TWENTY-ONE

SLADE TURNED SHADOW'S HEAD north by west, letting the big black build up his pace, for they had a long and hard ride before them. He glanced at the sky, noted the position of the stars; it would be full daylight before they reached the lake.

"The devils have a head start, but it'll take time to plant the dynamite properly," he told the horse. "With no flume guards to worry about the chances are they won't hurry. Maybe we can do it, feller; we'll try."

Shadow snorted agreement and lengthened his stride until he was going full speed.

After a while they reached the Vereda Trail and here the going was better and Shadow really extended himself. He slugged his head above the bit, stretched his long legs and thundered northward. But when the trail turned into the hills, Slade slowed him somewhat for the arduous climb. Shadow snorted protest but obeyed orders.

On and on, through the reaching chaparral, around dark juts of stone, along the crumbling lips of dizzy cliffs. Shadow's coat was glistening with sweat and flecked with foam, but he showed no signs of faltering. The east brightened and his flying hoofs drummed up the dawn. Slade strained his ears to catch the rumble of the distant explosion that would herald death and disaster. No sound broke the stillness save the soughing of the wind through the branches and the chirps of awakening birds. Now Shadow's eyes were gorged with blood, his nostrils flaring, but he never slackened his flashing speed no matter how hard the going. Slade encouraged him with voice and hand.

"Feller, I believe we're going to make it," he said. "Not much farther now to go, and so far nothing's happened. Maybe the hellions ran up against more difficulties than they anticipated, or maybe they feel sure there is no danger of interruption and are taking it easy. Keep it up, jughead, you'll get a chance to rest after a bit."

135

A final turn, the growth thinned and before them was the towering wall of dark stone standing firm and intact. Perhaps he was in time, after all. They flashed past the shack which had sheltered the flume guards; it was deserted, the door standing ajar. Slade gave it but a fleeting glance.

Around a bulge in the wall and up the steep slope, Shadow's flying hoofs sending little avalanches of stone rolling behind him. He faltered, stumbled, summoned the last reserves of his failing strength. Staggering, blowing, his flanks heaving, he topped the rise and Slade swung to the ground before he had hardly slackened speed. Three men were running toward him along the crest of the wall. Slade recognized the last of the trio as Rex Masters. His hands streaked to his guns.

The three opened fire the instant they saw El Halcon. Lead yelled past Slade as he weaved and ducked and took deliberate aim. The Colts bucked and roared in his hands.

A man went down, kicking and clawing. Slade fired again and again and again with both hands; the distance was rather long for six-gun work.

A second man fell, slid over the lip of the wall and plummeted downward to the rocks hundreds of feet below. Rex Masters came on, slewing, weaving, his gun blazing. A bullet burned Slade's arm. Another turned his hat on his head. His answering shots whirled Masters sideways but, his face a devilish mask of fury, he still came on. Both men threw down scant yards apart—and the hammers clicked on empty shells!

Slade dodged a slashing blow of Masters' gun barrel and they crashed together in deadly grapple. Masters was slender, and inches shorter than the tall Ranger, but he was all steel and whipcord and he knew every trick of dirty fighting. His fingers, like rods of nickel steel, fastened on Slade's throat. He fought with elbows, knees, feet and teeth. The fury of his attack sent Slade reeling for an instant. Then he recovered, crashed a blow into Masters' face that left it a blood-smeared pulp, tore the throttling fingers from his throat and his fist shot forward like the drive of a steam drill.

But Masters, one leg twined behind Slade's knee, jerked backward and up with the strength of desperation. That mighty leverage lifted the Ranger clear off his feet and crashed him to the ground on his back.

Masters screeched with triumph, his right hand shot forward and a deadly little sleeve gun spatted against his palm. He took deliberate aim at Slade's prostrate form.

And at that instant the very world exploded in flame and smoke and roaring sound.

Dazed, deafened, Slade staggered to his feet. In his ears rang Rex Master's awful scream of agony and terror. Through the whirling smoke wreaths he saw Masters toppling over the edge of a ragged gulf that had opened in the wall almost at his feet. Down he plunged, turning over and over, his limbs outflung, to vanish beneath the roaring waters that oceaned through the great gap in the dynamited wall.

Numbly, Slade stared at the frothing avalanche pouring through the breach. Even as he gazed, more and more of the shattered wall sluffed off, trebling and quadrupling the volume of the cascading flood. Far down the slope he saw a broken, battered thing that was Rex Masters' body appear for an instant, then disappear in the raging waters as the whole far half of the wall crumbled like brown sugar. He watched the mighty torrent foam over to the edge of the cliffs and thunder a veritable Niagara into the valley below.

Well, he had done all he could. Now everything depended on how well Verna had managed to do her chore. He estimated the time which had passed since he parted company with her. She should have been able to make out, barring accidents, but at such a time accidents could easily happen. Apprehension tugged at his heart strings as he gazed at the scene of devastation. He shook his head sadly; he'd find out soon enough. He turned to where Shadow stood with hanging head, his forelegs spread wide apart.

"Okay, feller," he said. "No use to hurry now; what's done is done. I'm pretty well knocked out and you won't be in any shape to travel for a while. Let's amble down to the flume shack. I don't think that is affected and maybe we can find something to eat there.

Together they slowly descended the slope and rounded the bulge. As he expected, the shack had escaped the general destruction, the break being well to the right of it. Getting the rig off Shadow he entered the building and rummaged about.

The farmers had not yet cleaned it out and he unearthed a store of staple provisions, a bin of oats and a large pail full of fairly fresh water.

First of all, he provided Shadow with a good drink and a hefty helping of the oats. Then he kindled a fire in the stove, set a pot of coffee on to boil and fried some bacon and eggs. After he finished eating and had lighted a cigarette he felt much better. Shadow had lain down to rest and Slade proceeded to follow his example, drowsing for a couple of hours on one of the bunks. When he arose he found the black horse up and grazing.

"Guess we can make it now," he said. Getting the rig on, he mounted and started the long ride to town.

Before he reached Vereda, Shadow had to wade a sizeable creek where before had been only a small stream. There would be no lack of water from now on in Vereda Valley, at least, for the springs which fed the lake would continue to flow.

With Shadow stabled, Slade at once headed for the Cowman's Hotel. The town was wild with excitement and was crowded with both cattlemen and farmers. Slade bypassed the crowds by way of a dark alley and slipped into the lobby through a side door, breathing a prayer against what he might or might not find here.

Then his heart gave a surge of relief, for the first person he saw was Verna Claxton. She leaped from her chair with a glad cry, young Nate Persinger bobbing and grinning beside her.

"Oh, you're all right!" she sobbed. "You look terribly tired, but you're all right, aren't you?"

"Fine as frog hair," Slade replied, patting her shoulder and reaching over to shake hands with Nate. "Nothing more to worry about. How'd you make out in the valley?"

"Everybody got out in time," she replied. "We were up the slopes when it happened. Oh, that terrible flood! It smashed every building in the valley to flinders."

"And washed away the crops," Nate put in sadly. "And they were almost ready for the harvest."

"Don't let it worry you," Slade said. "You have nothing more to worry about; take my word for it."

"Yes," Nate agreed, more cheerfully. "The land's still there, and plenty of water, and new crops will grow. All we have to do is scratch through the winter. And folks are being awful nice to us."

"You'll scratch through all right," Slade said, smiling.

At that moment Claxton, Jethro and Sheriff Higgins burst through the door.

"Some of the boys saw you ride in and told us," said Claxton as he vigorously pumphandled Slade. "What happened up at the lake? Tell us about it."

Slade told them briefly, for he was very tired.

"So the sidewinder got his comeuppance proper," growled Claxton. "Wanted the valley, eh? Well, he can have six feet of it, if we find what's left of him, the ornery skunk! Doc Austin told us what Webb said and we all hustled to the valley as quick as we could. But if it hadn't been for you, there wouldn't be many of the farmers alive right now, if any. A hefty passel of water came down that crack. Soon drained off over the prairie, though, and left nothing but a good sized river ambling along. Sure made a mess, though. Well, we'll see what can be done about it. Slade, how did you catch onto those devils, and why were they so anxious to tie onto the valley?"

"I'll tell you all about it later," Slade replied. "I'd like to have a meeting of the cattlemen and the head men of the farmers at your place tomorrow night, if you can arrange it. You be there too, Sheriff. And now I'd like to have a bit to eat."

A cheer went up as they entered the jam-packed Diamond Flush and men hurried over to shake hands with

Slade and congratulate him on his safe return. Old Sid gazed about complacently.

"I think it would be a good notion to turn this place over to the help to run on shares," he observed. "It's the best restaurant in town and we don't want to lose it. Jenks, the head bartender, is competent and he's already handled it quite a bit. What do you think, Walt?"

Slade and the sheriff nodded agreement. "I'll have a talk with Judge Cradelbaugh and iron out the details," said the latter. "Well, I've already et, so I'm going over and give the boys the lowdown on what happened up at the lake."

"And after I eat, I'm going to bed," Slade replied. "I feel sort of in the need of one. I gather everybody's being taken care of proper."

"That's right," said Higgins. "No need to worry about them."

Well-hidden under crusty exteriors, the cattlemen had warm hearts and ready sympathies. They opened their homes to the destitute farmers and their families. Already money was being collected for their immediate needs. All of which gave Walt Slade decided pleasure.

TWENTY-TWO

IN HIS LITTLE ROOM over the saloon, Slade slept soundly, to awake in a world all glorious with morning and with an outstanding feeling of satisfaction. Things had worked out much better than at one time he had hoped for. That golden sunshine, he thought, was a harbinger of peace and prosperity for the Vereda Valley country. Drawing forth the letter from the capital, he re-read it carefully, chuckling as he thought of the bombshell he'd drop at the meeting that night in the Cross C ranchhouse.

After a leisurely breakfast he repaired to the hotel, where he found Verna and old Sid and the Persingers, who would stay at the ranchhouse till they could build a new home of their own, ready to ride.

Slade and Claxton rode ahead, conversing, leaving Verna and Nate to follow. The rancher was full of plans for the farmers, to all of which Slade agreed smilingly.

Opposite the Diamond W ranchhouse, Claxton drew rein for a moment. "Guess the spread will be handed over to the boys to run," he observed. Slade nodded approval.

They rode on, charmed to silence by the autumnal beauty of the range. Far to the north rose a high ridge, like a blue line penciled across the horizon. Walt Slade gazed at it and felt his pulses quicken. And a Voice seemed to whisper—"Something hidden. Go and find it. Lost and waiting for you. Go!"

He glanced around at the scene of peace and serenity, shook his head and, a smile on his lips and anticipation in his eyes, rode on.

When the meeting was called to order that night, Slade produced the letter from the capital, glanced around at the ring of interested faces, and read—

"Sample submitted is Bauxite ore of high quality. Equal to the best Arkansas product. If deposits are extensive, capital here will be interested in their development."

Slade paused, glancing around. Everybody looked interested, but puzzled.

"What the devil is bauxite?" asked Sid Claxton.

"Bauxite," Slade explained, "is the principal ore of aluminum. Most of the bauxite mining areas in this country are located in Arkansas, where the weathering of syenite rocks have produced beds sometimes thirty-five feet thick. The beds in Vereda Valley are undoubtedly as thick, perhaps more so, and they extend for miles and miles. Bauxite is the product of the weathering of rocks containing minerals high in aluminum, such as feldspars. The cliffs which wall the valley are largely syenite feldspar and have undergone extensive weathering for a vast number of years."

"Aluminum, that's the stuff they make pots and pans out of, ain't it?" interpolated Jethro Persinger.

"Yes," Slade replied, "and a thousand other things. Those deposits are worth a fortune. That is why Rex Masters and Blaine Webb were willing to commit murder to obtain them. That is why they set the cowmen and the farmers at odds with one another, knowing that if a showdown fight came, the outnumbered farmers would be killed or driven out of the valley. After which they could have obtained the holding for almost nothing. They were both mining men, especially Masters, who was a competent mining engineer and geologist. He recognized the formation for what it was after he came here. But the farmers had already gotten title to the land. So he set out on a systematic campaign to start trouble between the two factions, an old outlaw trick but an effective one."

"And if it hadn't been for you they would have gotten away with it," Sheriff Higgins declared emphatically. "How in the devil did you catch on to the hellions? Nobody else hereabouts ever gave 'em a thought."

"Largely through one of the slips the owlhoot brand always makes," Slade smiled reply. "Rex Masters let me get a look at his library."

"Li—library!" stuttered the bewildered sheriff.

"Yes, his library," Slade repeated. "When he and Mr. Claxton and myself were riding to the Cross C, he invited us in for a few minutes. The shelves in his living room were crammed with highly technical works that would not conceivably be of interest to a cowman and could be understood and appreciated only by a mining man and geologist of education and experience. I had already made up my mind that somebody was deliberately trying to stir up trouble between the cowmen and the farmers. I knew at once that Masters or Webb, presumably both, were the only persons in the section who could read aright the significance of those cliffs which wall Vereda Valley. I had myself become interested in that unusual geological formation; it persistently called to mind something I knew I should remember but couldn't. Masters had already realized its true significance."

Slade paused to roll and light a cigarette, then resumed: "One of the books in Masters' collection was entitled, "Bauxite and its Derivatives." It clicked and I remembered what I'd been wracking my brains to recall. Bauxite! the product of feldspar syenite weathering. So I went up the valley, made a thorough examination of the terrain and dug a specimen which I sent to my friend at the university in the capital. I read his reply to you."

There was a stir among the gathering and Slade paused again.

"I'll admit," he continued, "that the scheme to blow the lake wall caught me flat-footed. Perhaps I never imagined that the hellion would be so utterly callous and ruthless. He knew very well that if he blew the retaining wall the resulting flood would very likely drown everybody in the valley; that's just what he wanted to do. It was too much for Webb who refused to go along with him to that extent. So Masters killed him and went ahead with the scheme. Well, I guess you know the rest. And don't forget, if Miss Claxton hadn't been willing to risk her own life to sound the alarm, there wouldn't have been any meeting here tonight for lack of folks to attend one."

"We ain't likely to forget," said old Lije Bixby, "or what you did, either."

Slade smiled and held up his hand to still a tumult of rising voices.

"One more little matter I want to take up," he said. "As I just read you, my friend in his letter says that outside capital will be glad to come in and develop the deposits on a share basis. That's all very well, but personally I don't see any sense in letting any of the profits leave this section. The farmers haven't got the necessary money to exploit the deposits, but the cattlemen have. So why not get together on a fifty-fifty basis and keep all the dinero here?"

"Why," said Jethro Persinger, "I've a notion I can speak for the rest of the boys when I say I think it's a darn good idea." There was a general nodding of heads among the farmers. Jethro turned to old Sid.

"What do you say, Brother Claxton?" he asked.

"Well," chuckled old Sid, "when somebody is reaching out a hatful of pesos for us to take for the asking, I reckon we'd be loco to pass 'em up. Right, boys?" This time it was the cattlemen who nodded agreement.

An excited discussion began, under cover of which Walt Slade slipped from the room. He made his way to the kitchen, where Verna and young Nate Persinger were preparing a snack. He patted her shoulder, smiled and nodded to Nate and passed out the back door.

"He's leaving us," Verna said quietly.

"Yes, I've got a notion he is," Nate agreed soberly. "And you feel bad about it, don't you?"

"Yes, I do," she admitted frankly. "But I'd feel a lot worse if it wasn't for—" her voice trailed off.

"Wasn't for what?" Nate asked, his eyes suddenly bright.

"For you, darn it!"

Some little time later—

"Well, for a man who says he never kissed a girl before, you do a darn good job!"

In the living room the ranchers and the farmers were still making plans and going over details.

"And Slade gets a cut, of course," said Claxton.

"He certainly does," agreed Jethro Persinger. "If it wasn't for him, I reckon not many of us would be here tonight. Where is he?"

"I'll find him," said Claxton. He went to the door, called several times, and got no answer.

"Oh, he's around somewhere, he'll show up," he said returning to the others. "Come on, let's stop the palaver for a while and go eat. He'll show up."

But to the north, a tall black-haired man, a smile in his eyes and a song on his lips, rode a tall black horse under the glittering stars to where duty, danger, and new adventure beckoned.

El Halcon was on the trail again, and happy!